FORTUNE: LOST AND FOUND

FORTUNE: LOST AND FOUND

Edited
by

L.S. Murphy

Kate Jonez

Omnium Gatherum
Los Angeles CA

Fortune: Lost and Found
Edited by L.S. Murphy
and Kate Jonez
Anthology Copyright © 2012
Individual stories copyright by individual authors
Cover Illustration Copyright © 2012 Kate Jonez

ISBN-13: 978-0615680132
ISBN-10: 0615680135

Some of these stories first appeared in the following publications: "Twisted Words" *First Time Dead Volume* 1 May December Publications 2011 "Hungry" The 7th Sin Anthology *"The Plagiarist's Wireless" Golden Visions Magazine of Fantasy & Science Fiction* January 2011, issue #13

First Edition

STORIES

A Friend in Paga by Brent Michael Kelley 7

The Bottom Line by Kurt Fawver 16

The Plagiarist's Wireless by Christian A. Larsen 30

Down the Pan by Phil Hickes 52

Trabajando Alegre by Wednesday Lee Friday 69

Things They Took from Luke by Garrett Cook 84

The Rules by Lizz-Ayn Shaarawi 94

The Second Vault by Andrew G. Dombalagian 102

Best Laid Plans

     Lydia Ondrusek and John Jasper Owens 114

Hungry by Eric J. Guignard 124

Twisted Words by Andrew M. Stockton 138

Storbeck's Gold by Cory J. Herndon 164

Gold! Gold! Gold! Gold!
Bright and yellow, hard and cold
Molten, graven, hammered and rolled,
Heavy to get and light to hold,
Hoarded, bartered, bought and sold,
Stolen, borrowed, squandered, doled,
Spurned by young, but hung by old
To the verge of a church yard mold;
Price of many a crime untold.
Gold! Gold! Gold! Gold!
Good or bad a thousand fold!

Thomas Hood, 1799-1845

A FRIEND IN PAGA

By

Brent Michael Kelley

Friends and a good night's sleep, that's what it's all about. As long as I have those, I'm the wealthiest man in the world. Before the Paga that would sound hokey. But now? Hard currency, gold, silver, oil— they've all been rendered valueless thanks to... you guessed it, the Paga. Friends and sleep, those are the only treasures left.

The old man takes another swig of liquid courage and paces his yard. He can take all the time he needs. I'm in no hurry. I'm honestly more interested in the once-pretty neighbor girl.

She's interested in me because I don't appear quite as broken as everyone else. I look rested. And I *am* rested. I feel like a million bucks. I have to make a conscious effort to look at least a little rundown, or nobody would talk to me at all.

She doesn't look me in the eye when she asks, "Do you like what you do?"

I shrug. "I help people." The words feel like battery acid pouring out of my mouth. Speaking the language of the Paga is unpleasant to say the least. Since the Paga came, it's the only language spoken by anyone, anywhere.

She swallows hard and nods. I can tell she sees the value in the service I provide. "But language is in the mind, not the tongue."

I nod. I want this girl. I want her to call me 'friend' after

I leave. I *need* her to.

My voice is as gentle as I can make it. "Can I ask you a personal question?"

She shrugs and smiles a little.

"Why haven't you killed yourself?"

She shrugs again, and her smile vanishes. "Why haven't *you*?"

The old man takes another swig and continues pacing. I can wait all day.

I tell her, "I guess I have hope that we can outlast the Paga. Maybe something that monstrous and alien is unstable. Maybe it can't sustain itself in our world. Maybe life will go back to how it was." It feels good to speak honestly.

Her eyes say she wants to throw her arms around me and cry on my shoulder, but her voice is steady. "That's why I didn't do it. My sister and my mom did. But I—"

"You want to see the sun again." I smile, and she smiles back.

We both look up to the sky and long for blue. Instead, there's the tan, veiny membrane of the Paga that encases the world. She sighs, and I know she's seeing how the sky was before the world went sepia.

"Come on, old boy! Come on, old boy!" The old man is stomping now, getting himself psyched up.

"What's your name?" I ask the girl.

"Anna," she says. "What's yours?"

"I'm Barrett," I tell her. I itch my right eyebrow.

She looks me in the eye, then looks at the old man. "Can I ask you a question, Barrett?"

"Of course," I itch my right eyebrow again. "I'm an open book."

"What did you do, you know, on the second night of the Paga?"

It's a bold question, and it catches me a little off guard. On the second night, the Paga spoke to us all from inside our heads. It said: *From each home, one must kill one's self to feed the others.* She's asking if I'm a cannibal, and I applaud her for it.

I tell her, "My oldest brother Frank answered the Paga and set himself on fire in the back yard. By the time we put him out, he was pretty much cooked. The Paga told us to eat him, and...."

She nods and looks down at her feet. "I couldn't eat my sister," she says. "I had some of Mom, but I couldn't touch Ruth. I just braided her hair a few hours before."

Since that second night, I felt sure that everyone everywhere at least considered suicide. If I didn't lighten the mood, however, Anna might run away in tears. It had happened before. "How do you know if the Paga has been in your kitchen?" I ask.

She narrows her eyes at me.

"It left the coffee pot on." I smile, and she smiles back. "Did you hear the sun filed sexual harassment charges against the Paga?"

She shakes her head.

"It's because the Paga grabbed one of the sun's balls."

"Those are terrible," she says, but she chuckles.

"I have lots more."

"That won't be necessary. Tell me, Barrett, why do you look like you've been sleeping?"

"I probably get more sleep than most," I say. "It's because I make lots of friends. I wake up every morning with the mission of making one new friend that day."

She folds her arms over her chest and bunches up her shoulders. "You're the only person I've ever met that can sleep since the Paga came."

"I've met others," I say. My right eyebrow itches again, so I scratch it good and hard. "I can show you how sometime. It's a little unpleasant, but it beats the Paga-sleep."

"I'd give anything for a few hours of real sleep." Her eyes plead with me. She wants me to show her how to sleep right then and there. She'll do anything I ask her to, but I'm not the kind of person to take advantage in that way.

And who could blame her? Since the arrival of the Paga,

sleep has been replaced by a violent state of hallucinatory hypnagogia. In that state, the wails of the tormented unborn saw through the mind like pulled barbwire. The howls of the freshly-dead harpoon the psyche and yank it in all directions. The Paga's tendrils dance over the skin— probing, violating, *stinging*. None go there willingly, but exhaustion always wins. I alone can resist the Paga-sleep.

"Can you show me now?" She takes my hand.

"No, but soon. I promise, Anna." There goes that eyebrow again.

"Let's do this!" slurs the old man. He hands me a bottle of vodka, unopened, and staggers around to the back of my pedal cart.

He plants himself in the seat mounted to the back of the cart. He buckles the straps across his chest and stomach. His right hand straps down his left, and you'd swear he's done this before. I strap his right hand and his forehead. His eyes are wide and bloodshot.

"Here it comes! Here it comes!" he hoots. He's understandably excited. A little relief is on the way. He swallows over and over. I hope he doesn't vomit on me, but it happens in my line of work.

I check the straps to make sure they're all tight. I put the jaw spreader into the old man's mouth, and I crank it open wide. He's breathing heavy, but he shows no sign of wanting to stop. I like this guy. What he's doing takes guts.

"Good for you, Wayne!" Anna says from behind me.

"Are you really going to watch this?" I ask her.

"Why not? Think I haven't seen worse? Just hurry up. That jaw thingy looks uncomfortable. Go, Wayne!"

He gives her a thumbs up, then blinks at me impatiently.

I grab his tongue with my special duck-bill pliers. I pull out and up. Saliva squirts from under his tongue and hits me in the face. When it's stretched as far as I can get it, I move in with the scalpel. Wayne's breathing is frantic, but the straps hold him tight. My scalpel slices through the meat in the back of his mouth. Blood squirts from under his tongue and lands on my right eyebrow.

And then it's over. I remove the jaw spreader and stuff his mouth full of cotton. His tongue goes in a jar of vinegar. When I unstrap Wayne from my cart, he looks like he's in shock. I help him into his house and lay him down on the couch and set the tongue jar next to him. I'm full service, after all. On my way out, I make a point not to look at any of the family photos spread across every surface in his miserable little house.

Back on the street I find Anna sitting in the seat on the back of my cart. She's turning the jaw spreader over in her hands and wrinkling her nose at it. The damn thing still has her neighbor's blood on it, but she doesn't seem to care.

She sees me. "Is alcohol the secret? To sleep, I mean."

"It certainly helps some people." I'm probably going to have to start giving her real answers soon. "It's easy to drink yourself silly and pass out, but there's a catch to doing that. The Paga hangover is worse than the Paga-sleep, and it lasts a lot longer."

"Oh, I know all about that. I tried it once. I just thought that, since you make all your customers pay you with booze, you might know a trick." She looks disappointed.

"Oh, there's a trick, all right." I reach into my pocket and pull out a bottle of pills. I shake one into my open hand and show it to her. "You gulp two of these before you pass out."

"What are they?" Her eyes are wide and desperate.

"A little of this, a little of that. Vitamin C, fish oil, opium extract." I shake out two more pills.

She gulps. "What do you want for those?"

"Nothing. I give them to my friends for free." I close the bottle and put it back in my pocket.

"Oh." Anna frowns, folds her arms, and hunches up her shoulders again. She looks back down at her shoes.

I put a hand on her shoulder. "Tell me a secret, Anna."

For some reason, she does. They all do. "These are my sister's shoes," Anna tells me. "She had them on when I braided her hair. She had them on a few hours later when she hung herself in the back yard. She cut the tire from the tire swing and tied the rope around her neck. Then she climbed up and.... I know she would have wanted me to have them."

Anna stretches out a foot so I can see her shoe. The shoes are black with red laces and a red sole. Somebody had painted a neat little heart on the side with nail polish.

She pulls her foot back. "Does that make me a ghoul?"

I give Anna a hug. "It means you love her. You're a good sister."

"Thanks," she says as she draws away. She wipes a tear and turns toward her house. "I guess I'll see you around."

"I think we're friends now, Anna."

She turns back to me. I see her eyes flick down to the hand holding the pills.

"*Are* we friends now, Anna?"

She beams at me and nods. Her smile is heartbreaking. "Yes, we're friends now, Barrett."

I hand her the pills and open the side hatch on my cart. I take out a bottle of coconut flavored rum and hold it out to her.

"What are you doing?" she asks, still wearing that weary, beautiful smile.

"Take a shot of this every ten minutes. After you do, read the warnings on the back of the label. When the warnings are too fuzzy to read, take one more shot to swallow the pills. You'll be out for a day or two, and then you'll feel fantastic." My eyebrow itches, but I try to ignore it.

She's on the verge of tears. "I don't know what to say!"

I give her one last hug. "Thanks for being my friend, Anna." Then I take one last, careful look at her face. I memorize every line and contour. I smile.

I pedal away.

Night comes, but there are no stars. The Paga's membrane covers the sky. The only lights are campfires, torches, lanterns, or candles. I'm alone, waiting for the Sandman.

In these moments, I always think of that first night when the Sandman came. Not that he ever told me his name was Sandman, or even that he was male. I called him that only because the Sandman is the giver of sleep.

What would you give to slumber peacefully? Sandman hissed in the dark.

"Anything," I'd said. Take anything I have.

What about your friends?

"Take them all," I'd answered.

Just one tonight.

I asked who, *who?* I don't know if I believed any of it was real. How could it be? But, in the days of the Paga, all horrors seemed possible.

Who, is up to you. Say a name. See a face. That one will go to the Paga to live forever. You will have your sleep.

"Bradley Bartels!" I'd blurted. I could see Brad's face with perfect clarity in my mind's eye. My oldest friend, sold out in a heartbeat for a few hours of sleep.

And then I fell into the most restful sleep I could imagine. No dreams, no tossing about. I awoke ten hours later in the same position I fell asleep.

That afternoon I felt a sharp need to check in on Bradley, so I made my way across town to his house. A tendril of the Paga hung down with a transparent sac at the bottom. Inside, suspended in amber fluid, Bradley jerked and tried to scream. His eyes were wild with suffering, but little barbs held them open. Vine-like tentacles held his arms and legs. Veiny cords crawled over his skin.

My heart sank as I realized the Paga would keep him alive in that sac forever. I wanted to vomit. I wanted to die.

That night, as I cried in the dark, the Sandman came again. I turned him away, just as I did the following night and the night after that.

But on the fifth night, I could no longer bear the agony of the Paga-sleep. Each night after that I gave up a friend to the Paga. First I tried to think which of my friends deserved endless suffering. That list dwindled quickly.

Then the Sandman hit me with a bombshell. *Who would like to sleep that calls you friend?* The question struck my heart like a poison tipped arrow.

"All of them," I moaned. Sobbing and wretched, I did the most cowardly thing I could ever imagine. I named them all. My friends, my family, my loose acquaintances. I gave the Sandman everyone I could think of who so much as knew my name.

I gave them all to our sepia sky, our replacement god, our Paga. The abusive asshole who moved in with our Mother Earth against her will, who won't let our real father the Sun have visitation rights. The Paga made us eat our own family members, and I gave the bastard every friend I had.

They'll never die, says the Sandman. *They all live in the Paga.*

"They're in pain," I say.

The Sandman chuckles. *You do not yet know the meaning of that word. But yes, they are in pain.*

"We're monsters!" I throw Wayne's vodka bottle at the wall. It doesn't shatter, only breaks a little hole in the drywall.

Monster is such a small word. Now who will meet the Paga's embrace tonight?

I picture her face. I see her sister's shoes with the nail polish heart. "Anna," I say.

My eyelids are getting heavy. So... heavy....

Maybe my special pills will ease Anna's transition. Maybe someday the Paga will wilt away and my friends will all be free. Maybe nobody deserves a friend like me.

The Paga wears my friends like jewels. Only the Paga and I know what treasure those jewels paid for. My cup runneth over. Tonight, like every night, I'll be sawing logs while everyone else fights tooth and nail to stave off the Paga-sleep. I say my little Pagan prayer.

Now I lay me down to sleep.
To the Paga send a friend to keep.
They'll never die, I will not weep.
I'm rich with friends and good night's sleep.

Who would trade *me* for just one night of peaceful rest? I'd guess just about anyone. How could anyone sleep knowing that? Easy. You never tell anyone your real name. My eyebrow itches just thinking about it. I try to itch it... but... sleep.

THE BOTTOM LINE

By

Kurt Fawver

Dozens of sparkling fingers broke from the earth, clawing at the clouds and straining toward ever greater heights. With the sun beating hard against the steel and glass, no one would have known. No one would have guessed that the monoliths were empty, that single rap against their sides might produce a soul-shearing peal that could spread to every corner of the earth. No one would have guessed that the skyline of the great metropole was dead, and these once-proud totems of capital ambition were now sepulchers for the very ideology which had raised them. No one would have guess that the power had finally gone out.

Yet, there the towers stood, proud and true, devoid of inhabitants and devoid of a future.

Save for one room.

On the eleventh floor of the Empire State Building, in an office that was formerly occupied by a small law firm, twelve men and three women, all clad in dark, crisp business suits, sat at a neatly varnished conference table. The names of these fifteen individuals were already inscribed in history books. Their framed faces hung above the halls of government and commerce. Their figures cast shadows over entire nations. Combined, they either owned or controlled sixty-five of the world's most lucrative corporations. They were the all-seeing eye floating atop the dollar bill's pyramid.

Fully prepared to slam plans and ideas against the heart of Western civilization until it beat again, these men and women had gathered in this place— not far from most of their usual offices - to ensure their financial legacies would not dry up but would pool wider and deeper. They hoped to dig beneath the substratum of conventional investment and uncover gilded, subterranean seas that could irrigate the land and swallow up the crises of any age. These men and women were here to plan. They were here to control.

An anxious hush slithered about the room.

A tall, heavily built middle-aged man with a cut-granite jaw and a polished smile stood, smoothed his fire-engine red tie, and addressed the group.

"The crisis, ladies and gentlemen, is beyond the scope of our projections. Almost seventy-five percent of the nation is without electricity. The remaining quarter is subject to perpetual rolling brownout, as," he waved a hand toward the city, "we all know too well."

A few gazes drifted to the windows. In the darkened boardrooms and vacant cubicles, most saw falling revenue streams rather than energy conservation.

Across the East River and beyond their sight— or perhaps just beyond the world they chose to recognize— dark gray tentacles of smoke twisted up from poorer neighborhoods. Below, equally divorced from their perception, West 34th Street lay in shambles, its surface littered with overturned automobiles, discarded protest signs, and mounds of refuse. On the sidewalk at the corner of 34th and 5th Avenue, an unconscious man sprawled in one such mound of trash; regardless of whether he was dead or alive, no passersby had yet dragged his body into the shade of a building where he might recover or bloat in peace.

"We simply can't get the requisite number of nuclear facilities up and running fast enough" the finely chiseled man, whom most in the room knew simply as Stapleton, continued. "There's not enough fuel for the construction equipment. And, even if there was and we could begin building, there would be too much competition from foreign investors. What it comes down to is this: without petrol, we need to make time. So, how do we accomplish that?"

Laughter erupted from a white-bearded man who was neither fat nor thin, neither elderly nor quite middle-aged. His eyes danced in shades of green more beckoning than all the printed paper stacked in the national treasury. To call him a slightly younger, slightly slimmer, slightly more well-kept brother of Santa Claus wouldn't have been entirely hyperbolic.

"Stapleton, you're an idiot," he said. "I've been telling you people for thirty years that we need to invest in alternative resources. Our fathers should've cornered that market half a century ago. They would've been heroes then. Goddamned saviors and visionaries. But no," the bearded man slapped the table, "they were myopic bastards like you. Now we have a depression and riots and only a fraction of the energy we need to lift our asses back off the ground. If we wait until we can develop viable alternatives or build more nuke plants, the country's lost. The economy will never recover without a complete restructuring. We're talking third world here. Zero GDP. Total infrastructure and market collapse."

A bald man with enormous, wrinkled jowls held up his liver-spotted hands and sputtered, "Wait, wait, wait. Wait, Calder. My risk management people say that substantial foreign investment could prevent that scenario for two to three years, and that gives us plenty of time to...."

The bearded man, Calder, dammed the flow of optimism with one dense, thundered word: "No."

"No," Calder repeated. "No more mortgages. No more outsourcing solutions. No more reliance on the Chinese or the Saudis or the Indians or whoever happens to be giving us an easy out. I've got an answer that will return us to the days of Rockefeller and Carnegie, when we could use the resources in front of us to produce results that were bigger and faster and better than the rest of the world's. I've got something that will put us back on top, forever."

Papers shuffled between portfolios. Notebooks flipped open. Pens clicked into the ready position. Hands twitched and tongues licked lips. Several of the gathered slid forward on their chairs, ready to pounce.

"We live in one of the most powerful cities at the center of a global community, Calder. Nothing you propose can stay within our borders for long, especially if your idea really is as brilliant as you believe," Stapleton said, a thin smile carving itself above his chin.

Calder shrugged. "Fine, Stapleton. Before I show you my solution, let's hear yours."

A series of gunshots popped somewhere below. Two mounted policemen charged along 5th Avenue, presumably tracking down more rioters. They tended to congregate on 5th, even though most of the stores along its length had been long since looted.

Stapleton nodded and again smoothed down his tie. "Well, I say we contact our boys and girls down in Washington and tell them to reassure the general public, let them know that cheap, efficient, renewable energies are being hurried through development and will soon be in their homes and cars, in their neighborhoods and workplaces. We have to make sure the public is looking to the future rather than focusing on the present. No eyes on today, all eyes on tomorrow."

Calder sighed and crossed his arms.

A woman with long, flowing silver hair and a conspicuous absence of wrinkles snapped her fingers and nodded.

"This," she said, pointing at Stapleton. "This is exactly the kind of thinking we need. Palliative advertising through government. Quell the consumer first and foremost."

Stapleton's eyes brightened. "That was the general idea. We need to increase consumer confidence, make them believe someone is holding the cards to solve the problem, that it's just going to take a little while to deal them out. Faith will buy us time."

The fluorescent track lighting in the room flickered off and on.

"Christ," Calder groaned. "*This* is your plan? You *have* no plan. Hide behind the talking heads in Washington until the masses calm down and some engineers magically appear to save your ass? Terrible. No insight. No forethought."

The man seated to Calder's right— an individual utterly unremarkable in appearance but for his deep tan and haphazardly puffed hair - held up a bronzed finger and wagged it in Calder's face.

"Faith goes a long way," the tanned man said. "I have a P.R. firm that actively advertised zinc as a rare metal and an investment firm that brokered deals for it. Within the first month of our ad campaign, we'd netted almost an even million. Three months later, four million. Eventually reports that showed how zinc was plentiful leaked into the media, but that was a year later and we'd made almost thirty million.

"Hell, we were *still* making money off that before the petrol bust," he laughed. "If you set up enough websites, plant enough comments in online forums, and throw enough ads on TV., you can create faith that can never be totally broken. We all know that."

Calder stared at the tanned man, slowly shaking his head. "The usual shell games won't work this time because you have no real solutions. You're all suffocating inside a bubble. Your ideas are trapped by a system of trade that's no longer functional or tenable. If we want to weather this storm, if we're going to lead this world into the future, then we need to get a collar and a chain and drag it there."

Stapleton sat, leaned back, and asked, "And how do

you propose we do that exactly?"

Calder pushed his chair away from the table, stood, and strode to the door of the conference room.

"Let me show you," he said, opening the door and stepping outside.

A minute passed. Two. Three. The bald, jowly man sighed and muttered, "This had better be good. We're wasting daylight."

Below, on 34th Street, a man and a woman scuttled back and forth from abandoned car to abandoned car, popping hoods and scavenging for batteries. Their shirts were caked in grease and their faces glistened with sweat. No one in the room cared to notice them, these two dark, shining ants combing for crumbs.

Finally Calder returned, leaving the door ajar. Two men in black fatigues entered behind him; they wheeled a large, upright rectangle draped in black fabric between them. The men stood at attention on opposite sides of the mysterious box.

"Here's our salvation. What I have under this cloth," Calder motioned at the box, "is a clean, efficient, environmentally friendly and completely renewable source of energy. But I want you to understand two things: powering the world doesn't come without cost, and saving the world doesn't come without sacrifice. So, with that in mind, I give you the evolution of business, the evolution of labor, and the evolution of power. I give you...."

Calder grabbed hold of the cloth and tugged. It fell away, revealing a large wire cage within which hunched a naked man, cadaverously pale and utterly vacant, his pupils eclipsing all but the slightest sliver of color from his eyes.

"Subject 138."

The man in the cage staggered forward, threw his arms out as if to grab at Calder's head, and bared a mouthful of chipped, blackened teeth. He bounced off the mesh cage and redoubled his efforts to reach Calder. Again, the naked man was flung backward, into the center of his cage, and again he lunged into the unyielding wire. The cycle of frustrated attack continued as Calder spoke.

"Subject 138 is the perfect dynamo. He will never stop. As long as there's a motivating factor to propel him, usually a food source, he'll continue to smash his rotted brain against his cage. I give you perpetual motion. I give you unrestrained energy."

Stapleton's brow wrinkled as he squinted at the display. "Maybe I'm being obtuse, Calder, but I don't understand. You bring in a junkie inside a cage and tell us that this is the answer to all our problems. How does a worthless, strung out meth addict help us? I don't see it."

Calder reached inside his suit and withdrew a small, gleaming pistol.

Stapleton shot up from his chair, as if to run for the still-open doorway. Several other people tried to duck under the table.

Calder held up a hand in deference and pointed his pistol toward the ceiling.

"This is not for any of you," Calder laughed. "Though many of you certainly deserve it."

"Do you even have a permit for that?" the ageless silver-haired woman snarled.

"I do," Calder said, dropping the gun to his side. "Concealed carry, issued by the great city of New York. It's a significant expenditure for such a base freedom. But, let's face facts, pieces of paper issued by the government don't mean much right now, which is, unless I'm mistaken, why we're gathered here today."

The silver-haired woman's eyes narrowed to slits.

"Point taken. But what does waving that thing around have to do with your..." She gestured at the man in the cage. "...specimen? Subject 138 or whatever the hell you call it?"

Calder snapped his fingers.

"Yes," he said. "Yes, yes. *It. It* would be far more

appropriate than *him*. I'll show you why."

Without hesitation, Calder raised his pistol and fired a shot into the center mass of Subject 138 as it charged the mesh barrier.

No one in the room gasped or tried to wrestle the gun away from Calder. Rather, all attention was pinned to the thing in the cage.

The bullet momentarily arrested Subject 138's progress. It stumbled backward but remained upright, never blinking, never grimacing, staring only at Calder. No more than a second passed before it ran at the cage wall again.

Calder raised the gun and fired another shot, this time piercing Subject 138's shoulder. The bullet had no effect; Subject 138 slammed against its prison, rattling hinges and wire. Although the man-thing's mouth worked open and shut as it clawed the barrier, no sound issued from its throat. Its active silence raised gooseflesh on more than a few arms in the room.

Calder stepped closer to the cage and unleashed one more round directly under Subject 138's sternum. If a heart had existed in the thing's chest, beating out hopes and loves and passions and hatreds, it was now in pieces.

Still, no one in the room raised a hand to stop Calder. And still, Subject 138 pounded on the cage, its abyssal gaze trained upon its assailant.

"My God," the heavily jowled bald man whispered. "It doesn't die."

"It doesn't even bleed. There's no blood coming out of those wounds. Look. None at all," the well-tanned man said, equally hushed.

Calder cracked a smile so wide, so bright, so full of righteous pride, that it was obscene on anyone less than a saint.

"It can't be killed," he said, "since it's already technically dead. It has no cardiac or respiratory activity and only rudimentary neural function. Any doctor on earth would have pronounced it months ago."

"How is that possible?" the tanned man asked. "How is it still moving?"

Calder handed his gun to one of the guards beside the cage and reached inside his suit. He pulled forth a small glass vial filled with a clear, colorless liquid.

"This is how," he said, shaking the vial. "In here is a bacterium unknown to science. Or, should I say, unknown to science save one laboratory that operates under the aegis of my pharmaceutical divisions."

"So... your people made it?" the silver-haired woman asked. "It's engineered?"

"Entirely," Calder said. "Nothing like this bacterium exists in nature. It infects its host and destroys most of the respiratory and circulatory systems. Miraculously, however, it leaves the nervous system intact but for parts of the brain associated with higher functions like reason and thought. It so happens that nerves remain viable because this little germ uses them. It releases bioelectric signals and, in effect, powers up its host after killing it. The reason?" Calder tapped the cage and Subject 138 swung a gangrenous hand toward him. "To further infect. Controlling the base nervous system, the bacterium relays signals to the host's damaged brain instructing it to seek out living organisms and attack them, thus spreading the bacterium to a new host. As long as the host's body isn't in a state of extreme decay, the bacterium will continue to propel it."

Subject 138 smashed against the front of its prison, as if on cue. An ooze tinted the off-yellow of rotten egg yolks began to seep from the hole in its chest.

"Where did you get him... er... it?" the bald man asked.

Calder shrugged. "A paid test subject. Probably a college student, judging by the age. Most of them were college kids or homeless. Does it really matter?"

The bald man shook his head and, jowls flapping, sincerely said "No."

Stapleton cleared his throat and waved a hand.

"Enough. Enough science. Enough about the little details. I don't see how this leads to energy production or economic stabilization. How does that..." Stapleton pointed at Subject 138, "... power all this?" He spread his palm out toward the city.

Calder slowly ran a hand over his beard and took a deep breath. He nodded to one of the men in fatigues. The man unzipped a pants pocket and produced a small spool of copper wire. From another pocket he pulled a board of LED lights. He wrapped the wire around a metallic hook on the lightboard then walked to the front of the cage and, as Subject 138 careened forward, poked the wire into the gaping bullet hole in its chest. Instantly, the LEDs blazed to life, a vibrant square of stars in supernova. The man in fatigues removed the wire and the lights slowly dimmed and blinked out.

"It's a living battery," the tanned man said, amused. "Genius. Total genius."

Calder clucked his tongue.

"Wrong on two counts. One, it's not alive, as I already told you, and two, it's not powering those lights; the bacteria are. The bacteria produce an extraordinary amount of bioelectricity, but they're extremely difficult to culture outside a human body. So much so that to replicate them externally is not cost effective."

Stapleton's eyebrows furrowed.

"Fine, fine. But where are you going to find anyone willing to volunteer for this? It's a death sentence. No one's going to sacrifice themselves for the energy to fry an egg or run a public bus."

Calder's smile beamed wider, more welcoming, more confident. Angel or demon, he was alight with the fire of revolution.

"They don't have to," he said, quietly. "We inject a few unknowing people on the street and the infection will spread far and wide. There's only one known cure and, as it happens, one of my pharm divisions developed that, too. We won't release it until enough infected have been created, of course."

The silver-haired woman nodded and jotted down

something on the notepad in front of her.

"I see where you're going with this," she said. "The infected will be dangerous. They'll have to be rounded up by the military and quarantined by the government. When we reveal what our science tells us, the talking heads in D.C. will outsource the extraction of the bacteria to us and we profit. The world finds its feet again with a renewable energy source. Eventually, you heroically reveal the cure and you profit even more and everything returns to normal."

"Yes," Calder replied. "And it doesn't stop there. You all have pharm divisions, too. The beauty of this bacteria, being engineered, is that we can reengineer it to seem as though it mutated. Then we release it back into the population, create more infected, a wider pool of resources, then develop antibiotics in *your* pharm divisions. Over a series of outbreaks, you'll all reap massive dividends. Billions. And you'll all be saviors, heroes, white knights of industry and commerce."

The tanned man rapidly rapped his knuckles against the table.

"This is amazing planning, Calder," he said, his voice speeding past words as though he was in the throes of a cocaine binge. "History books will write that we saved the world! Fucking brilliant!"

An extended series of muted pops disintegrated against the walls of the room. Subject 138 rebounded off its cage.

The silver-haired woman continued to write notes, but muttered, under her breath, "Must be turning into full-fledged riot out there today."

No one commented further.

Stapleton lowered his head and chuckled, an oddly menacing sound like a tiger's purr.

"All right, Calder," he said, cutting short his laughter. "Your plan sounds great, sounds wonderful. We start an... an... electric zombie plague, I suppose... and then we cure it. But won't we run out of people to infect pretty quickly?"

Calder strode to Stapleton and rested a hand on his

shoulder. Again, the saintly smile.

"Not in the least. I've had my people run the numbers. As long as the bacteria are periodically extracted from a body, they'll continue to reproduce until the body totally putrefies. Which means that our friend here," Calder pointed to Subject 138, "could, alone, keep this building fully charged for six to nine months, depending on how quickly he breaks down."

"Nine months?" the silver-haired woman asked, more to herself than Calder. "That's just enough time to...."

"Exactly," Calder broke in, lifting his hand from Stapleton's shoulder. "We'll make sure that the government will encourage everyone to have more children. Repopulation after the plague. And we'll pull our strings with the religious community. It won't be difficult to get the power players in that sector preaching the gospel of twelve-person families."

Stapleton began to chuckle again. He stood, grabbed Calder's hand, and gave it a single, earth-rending pump.

"You sonofabitch," Stapleton laughed, "you're really doing it. It's insane, but you're selling us a controlled apocalypse. I'm in."

"Me too, absolutely," the tanned man practically yelled.

A murmur of assent rose from the congregated.

Mixed in the chorus of yeses was a single dissident word: "Wait."

The bald, heavily jowled man raised a hand and spoke again.

"Wait," he said. "Does anyone have any reservations about the human cost involved here? I admit that Calder's idea is the boldest I've heard in months, maybe years, but should we consider that his plan calls for the deaths of millions of people?"

Subject 138's darkened, cracked teeth crunched together as it hit the cage wall. Part of a molar flew from its mouth and fell to the plushly carpeted floor.

"McDowell," Stapleton chuckled even louder, "don't

you own three fast food chains and the majority part of two cigarette manufacturers?"

McDowell, the jowled man, held out his hands in surrender and said, "I'm just putting it on the table."

"When it should be on the shelf," Calder scowled. "No act of salvation comes without strife and bloodshed. We're giving the world a plentiful, environmentally friendly, and totally renewable source of energy. We're saving the planet and, in the long term, our civilization."

McDowell rubbed his sweat-beaded forehead. "*If* your plan works."

Calder ignored the doubt.

"We've fashioned wars for far less than this," he said.

McDowell sighed and nodded. "True, true."

"So how much have you projected we could net from this?" Stapleton asked.

Calder, bored by the question of numbers, turned back to his dream, Subject 138. "Once the infrastructure is set and we have proprietary rights to the extraction process, anywhere from seventy-five to one-hundred billion per year. If it's an infection year and we need pharm distribution, add another fifty to sixty."

Eyeballs around the room went wide and hearts began to pound.

Subject 138 clawed at the wire, chipping already ragged fingernails.

The distant pops began to coalesce into bursts of firecracker sharpness.

"One twenty-five to one sixty, net, per year? Jesus." McDowell gasped. "I'm in."

"I think we're all in agreement. This is how we can maintain control," the silver-haired woman said. "The question is, when can we begin? And what sort of preparations should we make?"

Calder smiled, but this time there was no glow in it, only a chilled calculation, a godlike certainty.

Beyond the safety of the great tower, gunshots rang out

clearer, more frequent, more desperate. It was as though a battle had erupted near Central Park and was spilling ever southward.

Calder's voice subsumed the firefight.

"I've already taken the liberty of beginning the process," he said. "I'd strongly suggest everyone leave the city for a few months. Stockpile an ample amount of food and hole up by a beach in Florida or a lake in Minnesota. Then wait. Just wait. Let the bacteria flourish. Let the future spread."

Subject 138 pounded its cage.

"And if it spreads too fast or too far or mutates before we're prepared?" McDowell asked.

Without missing a beat, Calder answered: "That's why we have bombs, McDowell. That's why we always have bombs."

Everyone laughed.

The men in fatigues wheeled away Subject 138, still hammering at its prison.

And everyone continued to laugh.

THE PLAGIARIST'S WIRELESS

By

Christian A. Larsen

"Log Jamz, Portland's finest rock club. This is Gordy, man." The voice on the other end of the phone-sounded distracted, like the guy's brain was doing donuts inside his skull. "What can I do you for?"

The man sitting at the other end in a Chicago newsroom switched ears and almost dropped the receiver in his lap. "Hello, Mr. McShane? My name is Wes Thornton and I'm writing a piece on Wolves n' Sparrows for *Digital Vinyl* Magazine. If it's alright with you, I'd like just a few minutes of your time."

"Yeah? Cool!" McShane sounded upbeat. Then he added, "Sweet times and sweet tunes."

Gordon Raymond McShane was the kind of guy who would help you move a piano in a downpour, but he was also unpredictable, even unreliable, and rumors persisted that he was the reason Jimmy Sparrow disappeared with the Wolves n' Sparrows name in 1977, just as people were starting to really get into them. Wes had to know for sure. It was the crux of the piece.

"You must get calls like this all the time," said Wes.

"Naw, not a lot. Don't have the scratchola to pay for a land line at home, and I lost so many of those damn cell phones I stopped with those. You know what I mean?"

"How'd it all go down with Wolves n' Sparrows?"

"Unless you want to go back to the womb, I guess you

could say it all started with The Werewolves. We were the house band at the Ammo Room before it was the Ammo Room. It's in Chicago there. You know the place?"

"Definitely."

"I had my Hammond, the Fielding brothers, Axe and Garrett, manned the guitar and drums, and Pat St. Patrick played bass. We all shared the singing, but one night between sets, this lanky, long-haired Polack in dark shades plugs in his Les Paul and starts playing the blackest blues you ever heard out of a white dude. Jimmy Sparrow flat out yanked the stage from under us. That sound. The way he mesmerized an audience. He was the perfect frontman, but we didn't know the best part. Not yet."

"Which was?"

"He was a goddamn poet. Blew Morrison out of the water. His shit still stands up, even without the music. You ever read poetry from just one person that cuts to the quick of so many different points-of-view? I mean, his stuff was spooky. It was so good, you had to figure he'd burn out, but it just kept getting better. Hold up the *Clean Shot* LP against *Poppies in the Potter's Field*, or *Chicanery* and you'll see what I mean."

"Axe wrote 'Clean Shot', though. Your biggest hit."

"Yeah, he wrote that for The Werewolves. Jimmy loved the way Axe played the guitar, said he handled it like a weapon. It was because of him that everybody started calling guitars 'axes'. Betcha didn't know that, didja? Nobody does."

"I'd heard that, yes." He'd heard the theory, anyway.

"Hang on a second. I gotta let the delivery guy in." McShane put Wes on hold where he was treated to house recordings of bands that used to have record deals but didn't anymore. A minute passed. Maybe two.

"Hey, man, Les?" said McShane returning to the phone.

Wes didn't correct him. "Yeah?"

"I gotta run. The boss is riding my ass. I guess he's not

the Wolves n' Sparrows fan that you are."

"Wait," yelped Wes. It had taken him weeks to get Mc-Shane on the phone and the opportunity might not come again. "There's one thing I gotta know. When you guys broke up... what the hell happened there?"

"Shit, you couldn't have lead with that one?" asked Mc-Shane, sounding uncomfortable. There was something more to it than an antsy boss. "It was because Jimmy hated me, maybe. That's what everybody says, but I never knew we had a problem until I tried to tour without him as Wolves n' Sparrows in the late 70s. That little fiasco cost me my royalties. Didja ever hear how Jimmy got control of the Wolves n' Sparrows name? One night before a show in 1975, he flat refused to go on until the rest of us signed the name over to him. We had some really tough crowds, the kind they had in Altamont, and not taking the stage was gonna get somebody killed. He knew we didn't have a choice, so we signed." McShane's voice tightened. "Did you talk to the other guys about why we broke up?"

"Pat said that it was God's work and Axe told me that Jimmy went nuts or something." Gar died in a car crash a few years after the band split.

"Maybe you ought to ask *the führer* himself about it."

"I don't know where he is or how to find him," confessed Wes. "Some contractual clause kept everyone I've asked from telling me his real name or any identifying information about him."

Gordy snorted. "Real hush-hush, right? Like getting a plain look at Gene Simmons in the 70s— but here's the catch, Sparrow can't touch me because I'm broke. What's he going to get if he sues? You want to talk to him? His real name is Janusz Wróbel. J-A-N-U-S-Z-W-R-O-B-E-L. Tell him I said he can bite my ass for taking my life away from me; the good parts, anyway. Look, I gotta run. It's been a real slice, man."

Wes set the receiver in the cradle and leaned back in his chair. He slid the Wolves n' Sparrows *Live Against Death*

LP onto his lap and flipped it over to look at the concert pictures on the back. They were black and white snapshots, but they captured the band's live presence perfectly, with the pot smoke drifting around McShane's dense, curly lion's mane as he pounded the action out of his Hammond with his fingertips, and Pat St. Patrick, his mouth agape, plunking down a melodic bass line to match Gar's bombastic, but somehow jazzy rhythms coming from a cloud of hair and cymbals. Then there was Axe's crunchy, swinging riffs, wrung from a guitar slung almost as low as his knees. Jimmy Sparrow, looking like a cross between a rattlesnake and a long-haired version of Lee Van Cleef from a Sergio Leone spaghetti western, menaced the crowd in his dark sunglasses and black leather pants. He was the key to the whole story, and now Wes had his real name: Janusz Wróbel.

After a quick Internet search and a couple of phone calls, Wes found Jimmy Sparrow living on the outskirts of Chicago; not that Sparrow admitted it, but there was no mistaking that gravelly voice, even if Sparrow was only whispering 'go screw yourself.' There was no question that Janusz Wróbel of 50029 East Dunhill in Brickton was the right guy, and if he wouldn't talk to Wes on the phone, then Wes would have to go to him.

The wipers on the Honda flicked away the spitting rain as he hopped on the Kennedy, just a little too late to avoid the evening rush. Wes turned on the radio, and Rock 95.3 was playing Wolves n' Sparrows' *Clean Shot*, a clever-for-its-day acid rocker about motorcycles and sex, depending on how you interpreted the lyrics. It put them on the map in 1968, and unfortunately, it was all people remembered them for.

It's a damn shame how much people miss because they aren't listening, thought Wes as he drummed the steering wheel with his thumbs.

Sparrow lived in one of the unnumbered units in a turn-of-the-century mansion that had been divided into several apartments in the 1940s, but Wes didn't know which one, so he just started knocking. Rain ran along the zigzagging gutters and jagged edges of the house while Wes waited on the front porch, but no one answered the first door.

No surprise there. Everyone's probably still at work.

But the house was not empty, and the windows stared down at him.

Wes found the next door in back of the building as he trotted up the uneven cement walkway and, growing impatient, banged on it with his fist. Without a covered porch to stand under, his impatience grew and he hammered on the door again, shaking flecks of paint loose from the frame. Rain gurgled steadily through the downspout while Wes waited, peeking through the frosted glass in the door, but the house slept.

A flooding patch of grass separated Wes from the next door. The early dusk brought on by the deepening storm made the glow from the doorbell look like the self-aware eye of the HAL-9000 computer. It seemed to ask: "Do you think that's wise?" as Wes leaped to the concrete island in front of the door for his third attempt at raising the dead. He pressed the button, and the buzz died inside, but no one answered the door.

"Didn't I hang up on you?"

Wes jerked around, his heart caught in his throat. The man behind him was wiry, as thin and whip-like as he had been prowling the stage forty years before, but time had whittled down his long, dark hair into a silvered fringe over his ears. His chevron mustache had been frosted by age.

"Jim Sparrow? I'm Wes Thornton, from *Digital Vinyl Magazine.*"

"I know. You've been banging on my house for five minutes. What makes you think I'd want to talk to you?"

It struck Wes how Sparrow fully pronounced the 't' sounds in 'want to' instead of saying 'wanna'. In a moment of clarity, Wes understood Sparrow's slight but definite Continental accent in his screeds against the bombing of Cambodia on the *Live Against Death* record. He was born in Poland sometime in the 1940s, either under Nazi or Communist occupation, and he spent a bit of his childhood there before moving to Chicago. Given that English was his second language, he was a touch slower with his words than most, and more thoughtful, too, which made him sound like a lawyer, or even a college professor. Like he was about to quote Dostoyevsky or something.

"You're talking to me now," said Wes stamping his feet to shake off the rain, but Sparrow didn't seem to take the hint.

"What do you care about a third-rate band from thirty, forty years ago? Why not Shadows of Knight? H.P. Lovecraft? They were Chicago bands from around the same time. You might have more luck with them."

"They broke up because nobody cared. You had a huge impact on later bands with your underground sound, and when you were about to trade stardom for super-stardom, you just packed it in. I want to know why."

The rain slackened, but it continued to drip from the leaves like Chinese water torture. Sparrow's vaguely almond-shaped eyes narrowed, and he shifted his feet.

"I did some thinking this afternoon since I knew you'd be on your way over here, and I discovered something, Mr. Thornton," said Sparrow, stepping past Wes to unlock the door. "Do you know what that is?"

Wes shook his head politely.

"I need to talk to you. I don't *want* to, remember, but I *need* to. So come upstairs and make yourself comfortable. This may take a while, and you might not believe it when you hear how it ends."

Wes smoothed the corners of his smirk down with his hands. Sparrow was about to break into a full-fledged episode of *Behind the Music,* and while the story was bound to be interesting, Wes had pretty much heard it all, especially when he interviewed the redhead who visited Zeppelin in Seattle after they had done a little shark fishing from their hotel room window. Nothing could be weirder than that.

"Going up is easier for me than going down," Sparrow explained as he walked through the door. "Surgery hasn't exactly fixed my knee."

Sparrow led Wes up a long, narrow staircase to his second-story apartment, each stair pitched to a different angle. The parlor was a museum to a bygone age, with formal, elegant furniture made of dark woods and lush upholstery, original and well-kept with doilies carefully laid on each one of them. Wes didn't see a TV, but Sparrow did have an antique console radio in the place where one might be. The huge cabinet, made of real burl wood, had two knobs and six dials, like the eyes of a strange, alien face. Its mouth was a giant, cloth-covered speaker. Sparrow offered his guest a seat next to it and went to the kitchen to pour them each a drink.

Wes thought he'd better start asking questions before Sparrow changed his mind. "So... after joining Wolves n' Sparrows, how quickly did you record your first album?" He had to talk over the sound of the fan sucking the hot, damp out of the air in the adjoining room, in which Wes thought he saw a bed covered in rumpled sheets. Sparrow was either a very late sleeper or not as fastidious as he appeared.

"Too quickly," answered Sparrow from the kitchen. "Whiskey okay?"

Wes didn't drink but he said it was fine.

"We were signed for our sound, not our songwriting. As was customary for the time, we cut a number of covers hand-picked by the label, and we did a few of our own original tunes, but they were largely holdovers from my solo repertoire and The Werewolves'. Anyway, the songs we brought to the studio were either too much me or too much them. As a result, our first effort did all right, but not well enough to please the record company brass."

Wes took a sip of whiskey. He tried to stifle a cough as it went down his throat, but he only succeeded in making a series of choking noises.

"Went down the wrong tube I guess," said Wes, reaching toward the radio console to set the glass down.

"Don't do that!" warned Sparrow, rising out of his seat.

"Sorry," Wes said, bringing the glass between his knees with both hands. He swirled the whiskey to give himself something to look at.

"It's... no problem," said Sparrow. "Where were we?"

"You were talking about your songwriting."

"Oh yeah." Sparrow swallowed his glass in one mouthful. "We had our successes in the first couple of years, enough to keep us on the charts. Axe wrote 'Clean Shot' and that made that biker soundtrack, kind of ensconced us in the public's collective ear, and I contributed 'Bellerophon's Spurs' and 'Stone on Stoned' among others, but by the time we recorded the *Live Against Death* album, we were tapped out as songwriters. We made that record to keep the record execs off our backs. Our contract demanded two albums a year."

"Bands have it easy these days."

"Let me ask you a serious question," said Sparrow, leaning forward in his chair. "How were we going to come up with an album's worth of songs for our seventh record in just a few of months? Everybody in the group was wrung dry, especially Gordy who was getting too deep into drugs. The only one who was coming up with new tunes at all was Pat, and *his* songwriting was, to be frank, an *underdeveloped* skill."

"But *Poppies in the Potter's Field* was your best album up to that point, critically and commercially. A return to your blues and folk roots and a quantum advancement of the heavy metal genre."

"That's all well and good, but they were all covers," confessed Sparrow.

"What do you mean? You wrote all the songs except 'I'm Ready', which Willie Dixon wrote for Muddy Waters in 1954."

"Have you ever read the lyrics to the songs on that album?" asked Sparrow almost gently. "I mean *really* read them?"

"A number of times."

"Without listening to the music?"

"I guess so. Maybe. Why?"

"Well, what do the lyrics sound like to you?"

Thornton considered. "The anti-establishment cynicism of the proto-metal movement."

"Bullshit," said Sparrow, the corners of his mouth playing at a smile. "You just gave me critical boilerplate. What do the words really sound like to *you*?"

"I... I don't know."

"To be honest, neither do I, but to me they sound like the beginnings of the blues, bits of work songs, field hollers, shouts and chants. There's some white folk music in there, too, I think, and I'm fairly certain that the title track, 'Poppies in the Potter's Field', was a soldiers' song from the Civil War. It's about how opiates from all the corpses were seeping into the ground where the dead soldiers were dumped."

"Yeah, but you wrote it...."

Sparrow closed his eyes and sang the refrain:

There's poppies in the potter's field,
And laud'num in the wine.
There's poppies in the potter's field,
And the soldiers there are feeling fine.

"Arranged it? Yes. Squeezed it through an amplifier? Absolutely. Came up with the chord progressions and lyrics? No. I just wrote them down and passed them off as my own."

"That's impossible. That album is almost forty years old. If just a song or two was a lift, I could maybe see it slipping through the cracks, but the whole album? People would know. Look at Zeppelin. 'Dazed and Confused' was written by a jingle writer, and someone named Anne Bredon actually wrote 'Babe, I'm Gonna Leave You'. There's too many critics, too many journalists and historians to slip that one by."

"That's because there was a record of those songs," said Sparrow. "We don't know who actually penned 'House of the Rising Sun', but we sure as hell know it wasn't The Animals."

"Well, no," admitted Wes. "We know that much."

"And did Blind Willie Johnson actually write 'John the Revelator'?"

"I, uh... no, but those songs were still known a long time before you were even born. And how would you have access to Civil War-era prison camp songs that no one else had even heard of? Did someone take the time to write out the sheet music, lock it in a trunk, pass it down a couple of generations and then on to you? One thing's for sure... there weren't any recordings of stuff like that."

"Recordings? No," said Sparrow, his mouth curling at the corners again. "But you're not terribly far off."

"With the sheet music?"

"No, I didn't read the songs. I *heard* them."

Wes sat back in his chair, a little unsure of how to proceed with the interview. He forced a smile. "Good one. That'd make you, what? Something on the order of 160 years old or so? Are you going to tell me that you're a vampire now?"

Sparrow's smile was genuine. "If I were a vampire, I'd be like Max Shrek in *Nosferatu*. Too bad that was a silent movie. He could make sounds in his throat that would make your blood curdle."

"How would you know *that*?"

"The same way I've heard Civil War folk songs that no one alive has ever heard, sea shanties that never made it back to shore, and drinking songs whose authors passed out instead of passing them on."

Sparrow reached over to the radio console between them, twisted it on by one of the knobs, and then massaged the dials until the white noise turned into something intelligible. It sounded like someone speaking at a picnic.

A pinched voice squeaked through the hiss and crackle: "The world will little note, nor long remember what we say here, but it can never forget what they did here. It is for us the living, rather, to be dedicated here to the unfinished work which they who fought here have thus far so nobly advanced."

Wes shifted in his chair. "That's the Gettysburg Address."

"That's *the* Gettysburg Address," confirmed Sparrow. "There are a couple of different drafts floating around, but those aren't just Abraham Lincoln's actual words, that's his actual voice."

"Bull-fuckin'-shit." Wes was through being polite. "I get it if you don't want to do the interview, but why waste my time *and* yours?"

Sparrow kneeled in front of the radio and dialed in another speaker. This time Wes didn't even recognize the language, let alone the actual words. He crossed his arms. "What is it?" "I had to learn some Aramaic to figure this one out, but I'm fairly certain that's Jesus giving the Sermon on the Mount. Of course, he likely gave it a number of times, so there's no knowing if he's on Mount Eremos or somewhere else in Galilee. He probably gave the same stump speech over and over to different crowds during his ministry. In fact, I know I've heard a few versions, but I'm not that great with Aramaic, so don't ask me to explain the differences."

Wes was beyond furious and he could feel blood rising in his cheeks. He stood up and, unable to find a place to set down his glass of whiskey, he started for the kitchen. "Thanks for the drink," he said.

"I'm serious kid," called Sparrow after him. "This is the story you want, even if you don't want to publish it. I've heard 'Turn, Turn, Turn' sung in its original Hebrew and instrumentation. Early Brahms sonatas that he destroyed for their imperfections. Stuff Leiber and Stoller never gave to Elvis because they forgot to write it down. Jams that weren't recorded and were impossible to remember... you'd be surprised to find out how many really good licks and riffs, whole songs even, just slip through the cracks that way."

Wes turned around at the doorway, intrigued by the sincerity in the man's voice. Maybe Axe Fielding was right. Maybe Jimmy Sparrow had gone nuts, like Syd Barrett. "Why would someone let a perfectly good song just fade into oblivion like that, even if what you're saying is true? If it's that good, then people have incentive to preserve it."

"You're assuming that they *could* preserve it," said Sparrow, resting his elbows on his knees as if he knew Wes wasn't going anywhere. "How many songs were written by illiterate, isolated woodsmen, generations before the technology existed to record what they'd made up? How many drunk composers wrote a brilliant movement and slept it off before they could score it? How many rock n' rollers wrote something they didn't really like, but everyone else would have absolutely loved? You're putting far too much trust in the creative process. It's a fickle mistress, Thornton."

"How does it work?" asked Wes. "The radio. Is it magic or science-fiction?" He had walked back into the parlor, the slant to the floor drawing him to the radio.

"How should I know? I've had the back off any number of times, but it just looks like an antique wireless set to me. I've even taken a few classes on electronics repair so I would know my way around inside."

Wes walked back into the parlor straight toward the radio, where a faint whiff of ozone hung in the air. He reached toward that strange, alien face and ran the pads of his thumbs over the dial to try his hand at tuning in a piece of the past, or at least proving that the whole thing was a ruse dreamed up by a rock n' roll recluse. He could only find the whistling and crackling of static, like a storm of indistinct importance.

"There's a trick to it," said Sparrow, looking back and forth between Wes and the radio. "What're you looking for?"

"I'm looking to prove that you set this all up. What'dja do, wire in an MP3 player or something? Can't be all that hard. You even admitted that you'd know how to do something like that. Learned it in a class."

Sparrow shifted forward. "Look, Thornton. Why don't you tell me what you want to hear, and I'll see if I can find it."

Wes was incredulous. "*See* if you can find it? Nice."

"Try me."

"I don't know... how 'bout Shakespeare's *Cardenio* on opening night at The Globe, Pink Floyd's 'Have You Got It, Yet?' sessions, or all of Sappho's lost poems?"

One by one, Sparrow did. The acoustics of The Globe Theater not only brought out all the Bard's brilliant dialogue, but from time to time, an occasional cough or even distinguishable remark from the groundlings; Roger Waters' frustration was palpable as he tried to master Syd Barrett's ever-changing expectations in their final rehearsal together as Pink Floyd; and, though Wes didn't understand Greek, he found Sappho's lines to be equal parts inspiration and condemnation of his own clumsy attempts at verse. Tears rolled down Wes's cheeks.

It's like looking into the face of God. He wished he had Sappho's ability to turn a better phrase, even if it was only in his own head.

"Stop, you're going too fast!" Wes implored.

Sparrow's fingers worked like a surgeon's to hold the signal, but it would inevitably hiss and fade into oblivion before he latched onto the next audible gem. "I can't. It doesn't work that way. I can try again a little later, maybe hear some more, but it comes and goes on its own."

"Do you know what you've got?"

"Yes," said Sparrow quietly.

"Every Grateful Dead jam, every Classical oration, the closed-door debates that shaped the Constitution, the Rigveda... you have them right here. Right at your fingertips. Screw the web. You have them all right *here*."

The storm rattled the windows and blew the leaves on the trees pale side up while two men sat transfixed by the radio. Sparrow played things he had discovered through years of tinkering with the dials, and Wes suggested other bits and pieces of aural history. His personal favorite was hearing the dugout chatter during Game Six of the 1908 World Series between the Cubs and the Tigers. Sparrow preferred the musical snippets, but he did appreciate an occasional dramatic reading of poetry or prose.

"You know what would be great?" asked Wes, feeling a little drunk, though his full whiskey glass sat in the kitchen. "How about some James Joyce? Make it *A Brilliant Career*."

"I'm not familiar."

"Most people aren't. He burned it."

"Did he ever *read* it? Out loud?"

"I don't know. Maybe bits of it."

"Well, that would be all we could hear of it. This radio is strictly an ear into another time. It's a blind prophet in that it can't read or see anything. There are real limitations at work here."

"How far back can we listen?"

"I don't know if there's a limit on that, in the truest sense," said Sparrow. "But after a while the language becomes so unintelligible, even a linguistic anthropologist would have a hard time making sense out of it. I thought about bringing one in, but...."

"But what?"

"How do you share something like this?" asked Sparrow. "No one would believe it, or if they did, they might try to take it away."

"You're sharing it with me."

"You asked."

"Asked what."

"Why Wolves n' Sparrows broke up in 1977, even though there was every reason not to."

Wes had forgotten why he had come to Sparrow's house in the first place. Paying the rent depended on the answer to why Sparrow retired the band, but that was unimportant now. There were so many more stories to be chronicled. Wes could make a fortune as a historian, or absent that, a purveyor of military intelligence. It made him giddy. He was no longer a journalist. He was a fan of the mystery of lost art, obsessed with the gnosis the machine could grant.

"Why *did* you guys pack it in?" asked Wes, staring into the face of the radio.

"Because it listens to other times," said Sparrow. "Past, present... and future."

"You can listen *ahead*?"

"Yes," said Sparrow. "But as you might well imagine, knowing what's in store can be profoundly depressing."

"So what," mused Wes. "You broke up because you knew your drummer was going to die?"

"Nothing quite so dramatic as that. I quit the business of show back in 1977 because I didn't want to write anymore. I didn't even want to go on stage and sing, or sing in the shower, even. Do you know that when I hummed 'Poppies in the Potter's Field' a while ago, it was the first time I'd done it since I walked away from the band? I won't even play my songs on CD."

"Why not?"

"I bought this house in 1968 because it had a rich history in the Chicago music scene. It was owned for a while in the 20s and 30s by a fill-in player for the Wingy Manone Orchestra, and musicians of all kinds used to come in and out of here all the time, jamming together in the parlor on the main floor, and... listening to the radio right here, in this room."

"So?"

"So what if they weren't just listening to some live jazz on WDAP? What if one of them likes what he hears, performs it, records it, and makes it his own? I love all my creations, but I'd rather they didn't exist at all than have somebody else take credit for them. That's why I didn't just quit the band, but took it with me... the name, song rights, everything."

"How are you any different?"

"I know, I know," admitted Sparrow. "At first I didn't even realize what I was hearing, or what I was doing. Maybe I didn't *want* to. Then I justified it by saying that these people were anonymous anyway, and that I was just giving fame to a part of them. And if Sibelius didn't want his final symphony saved as part of the *Evolution* album, well, no one needed to know it, and he could still rest in peace. But when I realized that it could happen to me, that it could *still* happen to me... from the past, well, you know the rest. I quit the band cold and I've lived comfortably off my royalties in this apartment ever since, but...."

"But you don't have to do that," said Wes. "Who's going to win the Super Bowl next year? You don't have to settle for picking the winner, you can bet on the final score... and the beauty part? It's not even gambling."

"No, it'd be cheating."

"How is it any worse than stealing other people's inspiration?"

"Maybe it's not, but you can't always undo your past mistakes. You can only avoid making new ones."

Wes stood up and started pacing. It was what his friends called his oratory walk. "Mistakes? What are you talking about, mistakes? You could listen to newscasts, catch murderers before they kill anybody. Just how in the world could *that* be a mistake?"

"Look, I think we'd better call it a night," said Sparrow, snapping the radio off.

"This is too important...."

"I think you'd better leave."

"Natural disasters, wars, famine...."

"Don't make me put my foot in your ass, Thornton. It was cool to sit here and listen with you, but you're not listening anymore. It's time to go home, maybe think about things for a while."

"Yeah, I guess it is," said Wes, getting up to leave. "Thanks for the drink, anyway."

"You bet," Sparrow said to Wes's back. "Do me a favor and make sure you pull the door shut on your way out. It kinda sticks."

Wes stomped down the stairs, trailing his hand down the wall because there was no handrail, but he didn't make sure the door was shut all the way.

If he wants the door shut, he can get up and do it himself. It was a weird end to a weird evening. Sparrow had at been right about that.

It had stopped raining, but humidity hung in the air like dyed cotton batting. Wes marched to his car in the dense dark, feeling slimy in a layer of artificial sweat. It was a relief to sit in the driver's seat, turn the ignition, and set the air-conditioner to full blast without his girlfriend saying that it was too cold. It was goddamn comfortable, so he sat there for a while enjoying it.

I don't want any regrets. I don't want to feel like I do when I look at old friends' Facebook photos and I'm not in them, but that old nut up there is just going to hang onto it forever afraid to do anything with it.

Wes adjusted the rearview mirror so he could see his eyes. He was sure of only one thing: he had to do something.

His eyes slitted and pinched at the corners. The lights in Sparrow's apartment were off, as were most of the lights on the block. It was past eleven o'clock. The trees bent and sighed.

Wes switched off his car and stepped quietly into the street. He opened his trunk, unscrewed the light bulb, and pulled down the lid so that it wouldn't attract attention, and then walked back toward the sleeping, old house.

The door to Sparrow's apartment was closed, but had not snapped shut. The old storm door squeaked accusingly as he slipped into the true dark of the stairwell. He forgot to count how many steps there were, so when he reached the top, he raised his foot over an imaginary stair and stumbled into the parlor, almost falling on his face. His heart was in his throat, but he swallowed it back down when he heard the fan whirring in the next room... the fan and nothing else. Sparrow was still asleep.

The floor creaked a little under his feet as he crept across the room, his eyes already tracing the outline of the wireless in the muted glow of the streetlight on the corner. To him, it sounded like he was breathing inside a deep-sea diver's helmet, but his nostrils were only faintly whistling. Likewise, his footfalls were more mouse than elephant.

The console was heavy, but not exactly impossible to move. Still, he knew he couldn't drag it down the stairs. Even with the fan on, Sparrow was sure to hear the thumping. So he hefted it onto his back, where the weight was more manageable, though still cumbersome. He carefully tread back across the parlor and down the dark stairs. He tried to remember for sure how many steps there were. Doubt threw out phantom numbers, but in the end he reached the bottom without incident.

When he stepped outside, he set down the radio on the concrete stoop and pulled the door shut until he heard the faint but definite click of the lock slipping into place. Then he picked the radio back up and carried it to his car, where it fit snugly in his trunk.

Wes left his headlights off until he had driven several blocks away and turned onto the main road. He drove through downtown Brickton, past the movie theater and library, onto the expressway and freedom. He turned on Rock 95.3 and listened to a live version of The Who performing "Won't Get Fooled Again" as he merged into the fast lane, cruising toward home in the city.

A week later, Wes still hadn't been able to pull in a signal, at least not anything other than on the AM band. He'd worked the knobs and moved the console all over his condo, but had no luck, even though he spent whole days trying instead of going to work. His adrenaline had been pumping quickly through his system the night he stole the radio for him to feel guilt, but now his frustration was compounding it. He tossed a blanket over the radio so he wouldn't have to look at it, or so it wouldn't have to look at him with that strange, alien face. Whichever.

A few more days passed, and he started to wonder why Sparrow hadn't called the police. He *had* to know Wes had taken the radio. Who else would have broken in and taken it? Finally, his annoyance and remorse forced his hand to the phone, and he dialed Sparrow's number from the printed sheet he'd run off at his office, which probably wasn't his office anymore, or it soon wouldn't be after missing so many days and a major deadline. There was no answer. And there was no answer later that night. Or the next day. Wes didn't think Sparrow was the vacationing type.

The radio slid heavily into the trunk of Wes's Honda as he prepared for his drive of shame. He was going to bring it back, ask forgiveness, and try to return to his life, if Sparrow and the magazine would let him. The radio had already told him to go away.

The Honda crept down Dunhill at slightly less than the posted 20 miles per hour speed limit. Wes didn't even want to drive past Sparrow's building. He couldn't bear the thought of it. But there was nowhere to turn around and the street was one-way.

As he approached the corner of Dunhill and Grace, he noticed the landscape of the neighborhood had changed. Where there once stood a grand, frame mansion, diced into five apartments and badly needing new windows and a coat of paint, there were now only charred remains, jutting out of the lot like a hillbilly's teeth. A car was parked in the untouched driveway, and a man with a clipboard was talking with Sparrow. An insurance adjuster, most likely. Wes parked down the block where they were unlikely to see him.

The insurance adjuster had Sparrow sign a few forms, shook his hand, and then drove away in his own Honda, leaving Sparrow alone with his hands on his hips in the shadow of the untouched garage. Wes stepped out of his car and slunk toward Sparrow, looking as contrite as he felt.

"Was anyone hurt?" he asked.

"Thornton," answered Sparrow, apparently unsurprised to see him. "No, no one was hurt. Lightning hit the roof a couple of nights ago and the place went up like a Roman candle, but we got everyone out okay."

"Like you knew it was coming."

"I guess you could say that."

"Did you know I was going to, um, take the radio?"

"No, it didn't tell me everything, just bits and pieces. But I wasn't surprised it was gone when I woke up the next morning."

"Why didn't you call the police?"

"What for? It wasn't going to do me much good anymore, anyway. Like I said, I knew the house was going to burn down soon."

"Well, some good came of it, because I have the radio in my Honda over there. You can have it back." Wes felt stupid adding that last bit. Of course Sparrow could have his own radio back.

"Okay... where would I put it?"

"Wherever you're staying now."

"It won't do me any good there. It only worked in the house. In that room."

"It's over then?" Asking the question was like a knee in Wes's groin.

"Not entirely."

"What do you mean?"

"Do you remember when I said that I did some thinking after you called me the first time? That I *needed* to talk to you? I knew then that the house was going to burn down."

"Yeah... you wanted to tell someone the truth about the band? Why you quit touring and recording? Only somebody who actually heard the radio work would believe a story like that."

"Fuck the band. The band's not important. I wanted you to help me transcribe all the stuff we could find before the house burnt down. I was always more interested in the music, and not a particularly fast typist. I needed someone with a reporter's skills, a reporter's sensibilities. So I decided you were the guy. Unfortunately, that didn't quite come off."

"What could I have done in eight or nine days?"

"You were doing it already, that first night. I'm a musician, a poet. You're a journalist, a writer. You could have asked questions that I hadn't thought of. You were asking to hear things that didn't even occur to me. I know a week isn't a lot, not nearly enough time to listen to everything that anyone ever said, but we could have listened to some of it."

"I'm really sorry." The words tasted small and unimportant in Wes's mouth. He couldn't imagine how they sounded in Sparrow's ears. "If there's anything I can do to make it up to you. Really. Anything at all." He felt his throat constricting with tears.

"Come with me," said Sparrow, walking with his slight limp toward the garage, where he stooped over and raised the door, flooding the interior with afternoon sunlight.

Inside were rows and rows of neatly stacked boxes, labeled with Sharpie ink in Sparrow's precise hand. *Reel-to-reel. Jazz improvisations (1930-33). Unknown artists. Cassettes. Chess Records sessions (1950?-1960?). Chuck Berry, The Dells, Willie Dixon, Benny Goodman, Buddy Guy, Etta James, John Lee Hooker, Little Walter, Muddy*

Waters. Notebooks. Lyrics/poetry. Byron, Coleridge, Wordsworth, et al.

That was just the beginning. The cartons were stacked taller than Wes in tightly packed rows, like a government warehouse.

"You recorded all this?"

"Recorded, wrote and remembered."

"There must be, what? Years of stuff here, like the You-Tube of lost creativity. Is this what you've been doing since 1977?"

"Decades of stuff to transcribe and publish. I'm going to need some help, though, and this time I'm not going to act like its mine."

DOWN THE PAN

By

Phil Hickes

There are many places in London that boast elevated status because of their historical importance. The city is awash with them. There are the splendid homes of authors, artists, politicians and philosophers. Distinctive blue plaques tell us that these are places where inspirational artworks and theories first took shape. We can even go inside some of them and gaze at the writing desks and studios that sparked great intellectual and artistic conflagrations.

In the north of the city, close to St. Pancras, where great waves of commuters swell and roar, there's a listed building that belongs to a more prosaic part of London's past. Hidden away below the city's bustling streets by those prudish Victorians, the *Morley Street Public Toilets* stand as a monument to both sanitary craftsmanship and biological necessity.

It's easy to see why these conveniences have endured. Once down the stairs, which lead from the sign marked *Gentlemen* (ladies didn't urinate back then), you enter into a glorious temple of ablution. Its large rectangular floor is covered with an intricate mosaic of encaustic yellow, blue and white tiles. It's faded now, the boots, shoes and, in later years, trainers of fine gentlemen having dulled its sheen.

Along one wall, tall porcelain urinals stand shoulder to shoulder, gleaming guardians of modesty. Opposite them, six burnished wooden doors lead to the seated appliances, where a man might linger awhile with a freshly pressed copy of *The Times*, momentarily at peace with the world. Never has the euphemistic epithet 'the throne room' been so richly deserved.

It's not perfect by any means. The harsh perfume of chemicals and urine scratches at the nostrils. The temperature hovers around freezing, even in the summer months, perhaps to encourage excretory brevity. Inside it's dark and gloomy, despite the pavement overhead being inlaid with opaque glass tiles in a futile attempt to illuminate proceedings. And when the flushes and the sighs and the grunts cease, the only sound is the drip-drip-drip of ancient plumbing, which invariably fosters thoughts of a melancholy nature. The addition of cheap electric hand-driers has marred the Victorian opulence. Despite this, it remains a facility that shames the bland plastic and chrome restrooms of the modern era.

Its importance is further emphasized by the presence of Derek Mapstone, the *Washroom Executive* formerly known as the *Toilet Attendant*. His official job description stretches over two pages of the council's finest foolscap, but can be summarized as being responsible for maintaining the cleanliness of the facility. For seventeen years now, he's wiped, sponged, mopped, dusted, polished, scrubbed, and flushed. In the land of the toilet, the man with the bottle of bleach is King, and Derek rules his domain with savage efficiency.

Perhaps as a result of having had a front-row seat to the glorious diversity of human excreta, his manner is abrupt. Some might say downright rude. But then it's hard to think well of people when you're up to your elbows in effluence. The unique environment has influenced his personal appearance, too. His skin is pale and crinkled, a lack of sunlight giving it the appearance of scrunched up tissue paper. His frame is small and wiry, a similar build to the scrubbing brush he brandishes. His eyes are tiny black coals that flare up with an accusatory glow when they see any of the toilets' patrons. An expression of distrust, possibly disgust, has become the default setting on his face. When he does smile, which happens on the rare days that the scrawl on his betting slip matches the name of the winning grey-hound, it's not a heartwarming sight. It brings to mind the leer of the poisoner that watches as his victim gulps down their arsenic-laden tea. Or the sneer of the schoolyard bully as another nose is bloodied. When his thin lips crease up-wards, the joy is drained from the day like water spiraling down a grubby plughole.

He's not smiling today. For several days, the city has been besieged by a grim army of leaden clouds, which has hurled fat clumps of freezing sleet down onto the residents. The inclement conditions have not only cast a grey pall over the city, but have also dampened the general mood. Red-faced motorists lean on horns and shake their fists. Soaked pedestrians are ignored by ruthless bus drivers. The cats are scratching and the dogs are biting.

Down below stairs on *Morley Street*, the lack of daylight has robbed the porcelain and enamel of its cheery sheen. Hurried footsteps from above pound through the cavern-ous interior, a constant volley of dull cannon fire that makes Derek's head throb with pain. Drenched customers traipse in and leave dirty footprints over the floor. The grimy resi-due requires the constant attention of his long-suffering mop, which is now as bedraggled as the men who come in to enjoy a brief respite from the deluge. All day long he fights a losing battle against the dirt, until his hands are red-raw and wrinkled, as though he's fallen asleep in a cold bath. Even for a man accustomed to living in a damp twi-light netherworld, it's all getting a bit too much.

It's only half-past four, and by rights, he has another two hours to go. But enough is enough. It feels like mid-night and, even if a council busybody does happen to notice that he's closed early, what are they going to do - sack him? They're not exactly going to find people queuing up to take his place.

With a defiant clatter, Derek thrusts the mop back into its metal bucket and prepares for departure. A frozen pizza, a can of strong lager and a bit of telly in a warm flat. The thought of it is already lifting his spirits. He even attempts a cheery whistle, though it comes out as a reptilian hiss. As he's putting on his coat in the backroom, he hears the sound of quick footsteps trotting down the steps.

It's a punter— and that undoubtedly means another pair of filthy, stinking feet. After seventeen years, he's developed something of a phobia to dirt, so he simply can't leave with a set of grubby prints drying on his nice, clean floor. That means fishing out the mop again, adding hot water and bleach to the bucket....

Quickly, he drops his coat and makes for the entrance. If he can get the metal grille pulled shut, it's goodbye and good riddance.

Go and piss in the street with the dogs.

But he's too late.

As he emerges from the back room, a boy stands in front of one of the urinals, feet splayed, hand on hip. It's a strange but common pose, as though mastery of one's garden hose is something to be proud of. Derek glares at the boy's back, feeling the familiar swell of resentment bubble up like a pan of sour milk.

"Come on, hurry up, we're closing!" he barks.

The young boy turns, except that it isn't a young boy. It's a dwarf. And the little man glares back angrily.

"Go fuck yourself, I'm taking a piss!"

Derek feels a red mist curl its tendrils around his brain and give a painful squeeze.

"Well I'll just bloody lock you in then, and you can sleep in here tonight!"

Flecks of angry spittle fly from Derek's mouth and soar in a curved arc onto the floor, leaving miniscule specks of damp behind. An ant's piss patch. He scuttles quickly towards the exit, rattling his keys loudly, as though he's going to follow up his threat.

As he places the key in the lock, he hears fumbling at the urinal, followed by quick steps on the tiles, and then a loud Cockney voice.

"Lock me in, old man, and you'll regret it."

There's a menace to the man's tone that feels perilous to ignore. Derek's hot rush of anger is replaced by a cold shiver of fear. He turns to see the dwarf advancing towards him, and Derek notices for the first time the thick muscles that ripple underneath his clothing. The dwarf looks tough for his size with his broad nose, scarred skin and cropped hair lending him the appearance of a boxer. Yet despite the warning signals, Derek feels compelled to maintain an aura of authority. These are *his* toilets and he's not going to be threatened, especially by a man the size of a thirteen-year-old.

"Just be on your way or I'll get the coppers down here and tell them you've been threatening me."

He hears the tremble in his own voice and curses. Why did he have to mention the police? He sounded like, well, like he was shitting it. The small man smiles, acknowledging the victory.

"Just for the record, the police don't have any authority where I come from," the man says quietly. "Be seeing ya...."

With the threat of a return visit left hanging in the air, the man makes his way up the stairs and disappears into the gloom.

Only now does Derek realize that the little man is wearing exactly the same clothes as him, with the boots, black trousers and long, brown jacket of a council employee.

~

Fifteen minutes later and Derek still hasn't locked the gate. The encounter left him a little shaken, and he's had to sit down to smoke a couple of cigarettes.

The little shit.

What did he mean that the police had no authority 'where he came from'? Did he mean Tottenham? That's pretty horrible. Although there are lots of rough areas in London where the police keep a low profile. Either way, Derek hopes he doesn't come back.

It's as he gets up to leave for the second time that he notices a small leather briefcase by the side of the urinals.

That's not unusual. The punters are always leaving belongings behind. Not that Derek cares. It's a nice little perk. Just this month he's pocketed close to £70 from dropped wallets and forgotten bags, not to mention a nice new iPod that he doesn't know how to use.

No such luck this time though.

It's empty apart from a newspaper. Useful to break up the monotony of the tube ride home if nothing else.

Derek pockets the paper. The briefcase finds a new home on top of a half-eaten chicken sandwich in a waste bin just outside King's Cross station.

~

It seems as if the entire population of London is crammed onto Derek's Central line train to *East Ham*. A sweet and sour incense of sweat, damp umbrellas, and fast-food wraps sticky fingers around the hapless commuters. Shoves are dished out with abandon. Eyes are rolled in exasperation. Feet are trampled. Backs are nudged. Florid faced men in pin stripe suits perform impressive feats of origami with *The Evening Standard*, just to gain a few seconds respite from the carnage and lose themselves in reports of fiscal meltdown and political intrigue.

Derek is squashed in somewhere near the bottom of this steaming wreckage of bodies and bags. An aura of impotent rage emanates from his crossed arms and hunched shoulders. He should have known better than to take the tube at rush hour on a rainy day. Every jolt of the train sends him flying into another wet, snarling passenger. It's like being in a kennel.

There is a light at the end of the tunnel though.

At every stop there's a melee, as people attempt to alight at the same time as others try to get on. It's like a game of Twister, without the fun. At these chaotic junctures, Derek uses his wiry frame to sneak through gaps that open up in the human spaghetti, until he's right next to the seats, which are always jealously guarded at this time of day. His navigational guile is rewarded at *Bank*, and he slithers into a vacated seat just ahead of a flustered looking lady. She waits for a second in the hope that he might do the gentlemanly thing, but then she sees his thunderous glower and resigns herself to another few minutes of misery.

After reading an advertisement about cold sore cream, and ignoring an appeal to text DONATE and help Sudanese orphans, Derek remembers the newspaper he picked up earlier. It's still crammed into his pocket and he unfolds it to take a look. The title is unfamiliar.

The Underground Examiner.

He doesn't remember seeing this particular newspaper before, but there are so many freebies these days he's lost touch. The main story's certainly a little odd.

GIANT OF LOCH LEYN TRICKED BY KING'S SON— The Giant of Loch Leyn was today coming to terms with yet another economic setback following an audacious swindle by the son of King Llewys of Gwent. Reports indicate that the Giant, a notorious gambler, was persuaded to part with a large sum of money on the condition that he would be rewarded with a 'golden treasure contained within a magical casket without a key.' However, once an agreement had been brokered, the King's son presented the Giant with a duck egg, before fleeing on horseback. Servants of the Giant gave chase but were unable to prevent the King's son from escaping back to the safety of the Western Marshes. A statement was later issued by the....

Derek switches to the next article. It details a brawl at a tavern called *The Hanged Man*. Nothing unusual in pub fights, except that the article claims it involved a *'rowdy gang of drunken goblins and two barrow wights.'* The next is even stranger.

DWARVES VOTE FOR INDUSTRIAL ACTION— Leaders of the main dwarf union, the DUC, are claiming that over ninety per cent of their membership supported a series of strike measures as part of their ongoing campaign to secure better pay and working conditions. Celebrations for the Feast of Ullr were said to have been severely disrupted by today's walk-out, with many dwarves based in the service sector refusing to work. Negotiations aimed at breaking the deadlock between the DUC and their main employer, the Giants, have resumed after....

Derek begins flicking through the paper at speed. It's full of curious stories. Some mention mythical creatures that he's heard of, such as dwarves, dragons, banshees, and elves, but there are many articles that he doesn't understand at all. One reports the appearance of a Gwyllgi at a crossroads. Another details the development of a new hearing device that harnesses Coraniaid technology. Then there's the story about a boat full of elf fishermen that has disappeared, and is believed to have been the victim of an attack by an Afanc, which apparently is some kind of water demon. Maybe it's a newspaper for school kids. Something to do with *Harry Potter* perhaps? He's about to tuck it away by the side of his seat when he sees a section that makes his heart leap up into his throat and play a drum roll. It's below a headline that says *News From Above*.

TOMORROW'S GREYHOUND RESULTS — FRIDAY 17 NOVEMBER

ROMFORD

17.30

1. BALLINTORE BRAVE (6-1)

2. DROOPYS SCOLARI (3/1CF)

3. BOO BOOS BABY (5/1)

18.45

1. RAZZLE DAZZLE BILLY (9/2)

2. BIT CHILLI (7/4F)

3. HONDO BLACK (4/1)

He glances up to see if anyone is reading over his shoulder, a sly expression tip-toeing across his features, then pulls the paper closer to his chest and sneaks another look. Yep, today's Thursday the 16th alright. So this *claims* to show the results from tomorrow's races. Of course it can't be real, but even so, his heart continues to tap out a racy rhythm and a bead of sweat makes an escape bid from his right armpit. Glancing at his watch every few seconds, he waits impatiently for the train to arrive at *East Ham*. There's a bookmakers there, right outside the station. It stays open until around nine. No harm in popping his head around the door and having a look at the results. It's nearly six now, so he's missed the five-thirty race - if it exists - but still plenty of time before the last one.

As the train appears from the tunnel like a snorting, mechanical dragon, passengers on the platform see Derek's thin white face at the window, palms pressed against the glass - an exhibit in a human zoo. The doors glide open and mothers with toddlers are barged aside as he runs, for the first time in many years, to the exit. Outside the lights from the bars and shops daub the wet pavements with oily streaks of red, yellow, and blue.

A blast of gas-fired warmth hits Derek's face as he enters the bookmakers, and he inhales the stale cigarette aroma, ingrained in the sticky carpet despite the premises being non-smoking for years. A bank of TV screens give tired, anguished-looking men the chance to lose money on races in countries they'll never visit. Squashed Styrofoam cups and cheap plastic pens litter the worktops. Dreams of riches lie crushed in angry little balls of yellow betting slips. A buzz of commentary mingles with the desperate pleas for speed and cries of anguish as yet another fleeting hope expires on the grass and dirt of floodlit stadiums.

It's one of Derek's favourite places.

His raven eyes greedily scan the results. It takes a few seconds to locate the Romford meet, then a few seconds of staring at it, then about five furtive glances down at *The Underground Examiner* before the reality is finally acknowledged.

There it is.

The result from the five-thirty. It's exactly as the paper predicted. Derek's right eye begins to twitch, and he feels his bowels loosen slightly. But there's no time for sitting on toilets. The next race is up in twenty minutes and a quick check shows that all the dogs listed in the paper are running. He's only got twenty quid in his wallet, but there's a cash machine just outside.

Two minutes later and with the maximum amount withdrawn, his betting fund is up to £270. Knowing a little about gambling, he decides to place all his money on an accumulator bet. Slowly he marks out the names of the dogs, taking care to inscribe every letter perfectly. You can't trust a bookie. The cashier counts his wad of notes and, with ten minutes to go, Derek finds himself clutching his betting slip like the edge of a cliff.

Time slows. The clock's hands ignore his silent entreaties and refuse to quicken their stride. The buzz of conversation and commentary deadens until it's a monotone dirge. Unblinking, he fixes his steely gaze on the TV screen that shows lean, long-nosed greyhounds in Romford being paraded around by their handlers. After an age, they're bundled into their narrow traps, before the mechanical white rabbit comes trundling into view on its track, beginning yet another suicidal sprint past the slavering hounds.

And they're off!

A blur of fur. Derek tenses, every fibre of his body on red alert. He can't watch. He can't look away. His heart switches location to his ears and pounds on his ear drums. The race is over in what seems like seconds. As the dogs cross the line, there's an agonizing wait for confirmation of the results. Then, weak-kneed and trembling, he makes his way to the counter. The cashier looks up in astonishment and immediately summons the manager from the back office. No words are spoken. The slip is taken away to be checked. Derek can see the red-faced manager on the telephone, muttering anxiously. Close to collapse now, Derek grips the counter to hold himself up, until the manager returns.

"Congratulations, Derek," the manager says, "you've won 47 large."

"47… grand?"

The manager nods. It's the most graceful, wonderful head movement Derek has ever seen.

Ten minutes later and Derek's on his second pint in

The Ruskin Arms, his corvine features frozen in an eerie grin. In his wallet, which is clenched in his left hand, is a cash cheque for £47,556. If anyone were within earshot, they'd be able to hear him muttering the same words again and again under his breath.

Bloody hell!
Bloody hell!
Bloody hell!

~

Outside the pub, the Thursday night revelers are well into their stride. The knives are sharpened in the kebab houses, ready to begin slicing greasy strips of processed meat. The rain and sleet have abated, to be replaced by a bitterly cold November wind that throws plastic supermarket bags up and down the street like cheap streamers. Couples huddle together for warmth and race to the station, a red wine glow on their faces. Groups of young men and women defy the elements and stagger between cocktail bars in thin shirts and dresses, knowing there's only one more day of work to get through until the weekend. Derek is still grimacing at the bar, now on his fifth pint and considering a visit to *The Happy Ending* massage parlour on the way home. Everybody's far too inebriated to notice the small man that waits in the shadows, his steel toe-capped work boot impatiently kicking chips of brick from the wall.

~

The next few days are a flurry of activity, with Derek quickly putting a large dent in his newly acquired wealth. After phoning the council and telling them where to stick their job (up their arses) he takes a number of trips into

Central London, by stretch limousine, in order to peruse the swish department stores and tailors of the West End. Meals are taken at Michelin starred restaurants. Vintage wines are slurped, and Cuban cigars puffed. *The Happy Ending* also records a small but significant rise in its profits. A queue of delivery trucks pull up outside Derek's modest flat to deliver a succession of items: a 103 inch HD TV and home entertainment system, a new leather suite, a King-size bed complete with ergonomic mattress and goose down bedclothes, an Afghan rug from Harrods. Neighbours are also surprised to see him sporting a shiny purple Versace track suit and spotless white loafers. A new sheepskin coat and trilby add the finishing touches to this sartorially groundbreaking ensemble.

All of which should be great.

But there's something bothering him.

And it's spoiling his fun.

For starters, there's the source of his newfound wealth— the newspaper from the toilets. Where did it come from? What does it all mean? Is there really another world in which giants exist and people can see into the future? Not having ever bothered to consider the metaphysical make-up of the universe, he finds himself in unfamiliar and uncomfortable territory.

It makes his head hurt.

Even more unsettling is the feeling he's being watched. As he walks the streets of London he can sense someone lurking behind him. Invisible eyes watch his every move. A small dark shadow flits in and out at the edges of his vision. Worse, he hears slow footsteps walking past his window late in the evening. Last night there was even the sound of someone scrabbling at the lock on his front door. He didn't dare get up to check, but stayed buried in the comforting warmth of his new eiderdown, wide eyes staring into darkness, until the noise abated.

He thinks he knows who it is, too. Didn't the little chap in the toilet insinuate that he'd be seeing him again? Surely it's too much of a coincidence that the same day he has an altercation with a dwarf, he finds himself reading about them in some weird newspaper? He has a horrible feeling that something unpleasant is lurking around the corner. Not even his new cinematic screen can dispel the needles of anxiety that prick behind his small, watery eyes.

There's no doubt about it, the shit's about to hit the fan.

~

A few days later, Derek's new bedside clock is showing 3:47 a.m. when the phone rings. Immediately he burrows back into the pillow, willing it to stop. Nothing good ever comes from a call in the middle of the night. But five minutes later, he lifts the receiver from its cradle and whispers a tentative, "hello?"

"So, enjoying yourself are ya?" says a cockney voice that sounds horribly familiar.

"Who's this?" Derek replies, as though feigning ignorance might somehow get him off the hook.

"The name's Digger, but I think you know who I am. You've been a naughty boy, haven't ya?"

"I don't know what you're talking about."

"Keep playing me for a fool, Mapstone, and you'll pay the price," the voice warns. "I know where you live... now."

Derek's heart is fluttering, and a cold sheen of sweat wraps itself around him like an icy cloak.

"H-how do you know my name?"

"I've been following ya, haven't I," the voice growls. "Been finding out all there is to know about you since you nicked my briefcase. I want to talk to you, Mapstone, face to face."

"I'd love to, Mr. Digger, really I would," Derek says, "but I'm leaving the country tomorrow for a couple of weeks in Spain, so it'll have to wait until I get back. Sorry 'bout that.

Bye!"

Derek slams down the phone and wheezes with relief.

He's just on his way to grab his suitcase when the front door flies off its hinges.

A small silhouette, no more than four feet high, stands in the doorway.

"You ain't going anywhere, sunshine."

~

Derek discovers that it's hard to concentrate with a knife at your throat. Up close he can see fine indentations on the edge of the blade. By the look of it, it's been sharpened very recently. Although he can't take his eyes off the blade, he's aware of the small man on the other end.

"So, ready for our little chat now?"

"Um... yes, that would be great." Derek gulps. "Perhaps it would be easier if you put down the knife though— would you like a cup of tea?"

A few minutes later and Derek's diminutive visitor sits on his new leather suite with a mug of tea. The knife lies on the glass coffee table between them, a sinister third guest. The minimal glow from the shiny *John Lewis* lamp in the corner emphasizes the scars and pockmarks on Digger's face.

"You see, you've gone and landed yourself in the proverbial," Diggers says.

"Why, what have I done?"

"Oh, don't be an idiot. Regularly find newspapers giving you the greyhound results do ya? We get them down below because the wood elves like popping up for a flutter every now and then. Well, you know what they're like when it comes to gambling."

"Er... yeah." Derek says.

"So I picked up the paper on my way upstairs. Had a day off. Well, officially we were on strike, but either way, it meant I didn't have to work. I didn't have anything on, so thought I'd pop up and have a look at the famous *Morley Street* conveniences, just a quick nose around like."

Derek's confused.

"What do you mean upstairs? Where do you come from? And why would you want to come and look at a toilet?"

"Upstairs - that's what we call where you lot live. We're from down below, see?"

Derek can't see, but nods along anyway.

"And I wanted to have a look at *Morley Street* 'cos I've heard a lot about it, what with being in the same line of work and that."

"Really?"

Digger nods, a look of pride on his face.

"Like my old Dad before me and his before that. As I was saying, only meant to pop in for a quick look, but of course I had to have a piss once I was there, just to tell the lads back at work that I'd taken a leak at *Morley Street*. But you had to come along and start hurrying me up, didn't ya? Next thing I know I'm on my way back downstairs and I suddenly think, 'where's me case?' By the time I got back, the gates were locked and I had to find it before you took advantage of certain information what's not to meant to be seen by those above ground. But I was too late, wasn't I? And now you've gone and broken the rules."

A dark look crosses Digger's face, and Derek suddenly feels nervous again.

"So... I want that money what you won on them dogs."

Derek spits a mouthful of Ceylon over his new rug.

"But I've spent most of it already! You can't have it back now!" he cries.

"I was afraid you'd say that," Digger says, leaning over to pick up the knife.

~

Ironically, the journey to the underground starts at the Underground station. Once all the passers-by have passed by, Digger unlocks one of the old service lifts and inserts a large rusty key. Ushering Derek inside with his knife, he closes the doors and opens up a panel. There's a line of buttons numbering from 1 to 174. Digger presses number 174 and the doors close with a metallic rattle.

As the light from the station fades, Derek fights a rising sense of panic. His teeth chatter, though whether from fear or the sudden drop in temperature, he's not sure.

"So j-just the one job, you say, D-Digger?"

"Yep, just a quick job, and then we're all square and you can get back up top and enjoy all that lovely money."

"And... what is it exactly?"

Digger grins, and Derek notices for the first time that he has a gold front tooth.

"You'll see."

Ten agonizing minutes later, the lift bumps to a stop and Digger flings open the doors, before gesturing theatrically.

Derek staggers back as an arctic blast hits him squarely on the jaw. Before him a grey, treeless wasteland stretches off into the distance. Shimmering tapestries of black rain glide across it. Dark clouds glower from above. It's like Tottenham on a January evening.

But the most striking feature of the landscape isn't natural. Before him is a tower of impossibly huge dimensions, made from stone blocks, each as big as a house. Derek cranes his scrawny neck upwards, but he still can't see the top of it, which stretches off into the clouds. There's a massive wooden door on one side, made from planks as long as oak trees and painted a dull blue. On it is a sign, with *Gentlemen* written on it in large Gothic lettering.

Digger hands Derek a small scrubbing brush and a bottle of bleach.

"Right then, Mapstone," says Digger. "What you do know about Giant shit?"

TRABAJANDO ALEGRE

By

Wednesday Lee Friday

I didn't know what the hell I was gonna say to her. She was sitting on the porch when I pulled up, looking beautiful and sad. One look at me and Cara knew. Felix sat next to her wearing a kid-sized green army helmet. He saluted me as I got out of the car. Before I could say anything, my fiancée reached behind her son to pick up a suitcase. A *suitcase*. Just like that.

"Cara, can't we just—"

"I didn't want to leave without seeing you in person. Felix wanted to say goodbye." Bright green eyes full of tears as if this wasn't her decision. It was. Her hair was long and dark, a wig shop once offered my weeks wage for that hair. Now she ran her fingers through it nervously, pushing it out of her face. The little man ran forward and hugged me around the waist. His helmet tilted sideways and fell to the ground with a tiny crash.

"I'll miss you, Uncle Paulo. I don't want to go back to Ernie's." He sniffled like he was going to cry, but stopped himself. That prick Ernie once told Felix with a smack that *only pussyboys cried*.

"Ernie?" I said, and then lowered my voice so the kid wouldn't hear. "What the hell do you think you're doing? Ernie *hit* you. In front of Felix! You're leaving everything we've built together to go back to *that*?"

Cara must have known she was wrong. She couldn't

even meet my eye.

"Ernesto never hit Felix, only me. He's gotten counseling, and a new job. He says he's better. And he can... he can take care of Felix and me." She looked at the ground. "I'm sorry. Really."

My gut was heavy and trembling, like it might collapse into itself at any moment. "When are you... when?"

"Bank says I gotta have everything out by the end of the week. Guy actually said they've been *more than patient* with us. Like I didn't pay the mortgage because I'm just being difficult. Like it's my fault that idiot Tipton can't run a business worth a damn." Tipton paid me under the table for the last eight years. When he laid me off, I couldn't even apply for unemployment. Figures. He breaks the law and I'm the one who suffers.

"Come on, Felix," Cara said, barely audible.

His grip moved from my waist to my leg, where it tightened. "I don't want to go, Uncle Paulo. Can't I stay here with you?"

Poor kid.

"Come *on* Felix!" His mother badgered him into the backseat, and waited for him to buckle up. Without so much as a backward glance, they left me.

"Dunno what you're complaining about, amigo," Tito passed the joint as he explained his philosophy. "Yeah, you lost the girl, but it don't cost you a cent. No big wedding to pay for, no alimony, child support— none of that shit." In his marijuana haze he didn't seem to realize that I had no house, no family, no job. Just my oldest friend Tito, and a photo of Cara and Felix taken at the zoo. They grinned with genuine joy, wearing silly foam hats in the shape of green spotted frogs.

"It's too bad you didn't sign up with *Trabajando Alegre*. I'm telling you, amigo, it's the best thing the white man has ever done for us." He smirked, and I couldn't tell whether or not he was screwing with me.

"I wouldn't get involved with that shit even if I could. I don't need anyone's help finding a job feeding pigs and pulling plows like a goddamn mule. You telling me to get the same job as some illiterate high school dropout?"

"Calmate, Amigo. That's not what I'm saying. You know what it says on the signs: *Feed the Poor, Serve the Community*, all that shit. Miguel Managua joined up— him and his sister. They got placed in some fancy-ass restaurant and now they send $1,200 home to their family every month."

That couldn't be. Twelve hundred dollars a month *after* living expenses? How was that possible?

"Miguel said they have physical therapy. He tore a muscle and they sent some old lady to massage it every night." Tito exhaled.

"You believe that crap? There's a government program for uneducated Latinos that gives out foot rubs every night? What next? Therapeutic happy endings?"

"It's really too bad they wouldn't take you, man. They mostly take ESL students, and you grew up on English. Plus it's kind of like the military in Mexico— they don't want you if you're too smart. Miguel lied and said he had a GED. Nobody checked."

Babble Babble, I wished he would just shut up.

Mrs. Bee was the head librarian. She was nice enough to let me do a quick wash-up at the Mallard Creek Library branch in the mornings, after I started living in my Escort. Felix and I used to come for story hour they had in the mornings before he started kindergarten. Cara said he was too young to see *The Hobbit* when they played it on the old film projector, but the boy begged for a week and she finally agreed. Mrs. Bee was always kind to Felix, and less moody than his mother.

I stayed at the library for the next three mornings, combing through the job listings every place I could find them, newspapers, bulletin boards, the Internet. I made calls, sent resumes from the public computers, checked my email every few minutes. Nothing. Not a nibble.

The fourth morning, I came out of the library restroom with freshly brushed teeth and a foreboding feeling in my gut.

"Paul, I need you to come with me please." I was sure Mrs. Bee was gonna tell me I couldn't hang around all morning anymore. I couldn't blame her. But she didn't. It was much worse.

"I want to caution you that this might be very upsetting. I need you to stay calm, okay?"

My god. *What?* I wanted to scream at her. *Just tell me!* I nodded, but didn't say a word. She led me to her office.

Felix. His arm in a sling, left side of his face bruised. His eyes widened when he glanced up at me, still wearing his green army helmet.

"I'm sorry, Uncle Paolo. I couldn't go to school. Ernie is bad! Mommy got in trouble and he—"

I knelt down and hugged him as he dissolved into tears. Goddamn Cara. No. Goddamn Ernie, that sonofabitch. I could kill him with my own hands, I swear. But who would that help?

"It's gonna be okay, little man. I'm not mad. Is your mom at Ernie's? Is he with her?"

He shook his head. Mrs. Bee explained that Cara and Ernie had both been arrested when a neighbor called the police about their fighting. *Their* fighting. What idiot cop would believe Cara was hitting *him?*

"Felix hid under the bed, and apparently no one even knew to look for him," she said quietly. "His mother is being released later today. I can keep him until then."

I looked at her with profoundest gratitude.

"How did you know to come here, little guy?" I asked Felix after he wiped away his tears.

"I knew Mrs. Bee would help me."

The librarian made a small choking sound and sniffled.

Mrs. Bee let Felix stay at the Mallard Creek branch reading, and drinking juice. I left to do the only thing I could think of. Not for me— for Felix. Somebody had to look out for that kid.

"Welcome to Trabajando Alegre," the lily-white woman at the admitting desk spoke in a singsong tone. "Good people doing good work, feeding the poor and serving the community. I'm so glad you came in today!" Her pale face was made up like a doll mi prima, mama's niece Angela, used to have.

The bright white lights in the room made the lady look like porcelain. The space was open and huge with cameras everywhere, giving the distinct impression that nothing happened here in secret. The porcelain pink woman leaned in and smiled again. Speaking slowly she said, "Do you speak English?"

"Yeah, um... Julia." I said, noticing her nametag. "I'm uh... I came to see if you were hiring, or whatever you call it. My name is—"

"We can get your details sorted out after you've seen our welcome video. English presentation is held in room four." Julia reached under the desk as she nodded, indicating that I should turn around. A blue '4' lit up on the far door, and then was gone.

Julia handed me a clipboard full of papers with a shiny, colored pamphlet on top. The vibe here was bright and happy— obscenely so. Enormous banners indicated separate departments apparently signified by different colored uniforms, white, blue, and red. Workers wore fixed grins as they carted stacks of boxes on dollies or carried silver covered trays to the elevators. I went through the far door like they told me.

After less than a minute of waiting in my seat, the lights went low in the tiny theatre, and curtains opened up to reveal a movie screen. I looked behind me, no one else here. Horrible 80's synth guitar music started. Stock footage of factories and brown people working in fields laid the background for a heavily accented but English-speaking narrator.

"¡Trabajando Alegre! Feeding the Hungry. Serving the Community. Since its inception, the Trabajando Alegre program has provided employment, housing and daily needs to countless immigrants to America. Building neighborhoods that thrive, and training you for a better future!" This was probably a great opportunity for people who actually had GEDs, or less. I felt like a fraud.

"Trabajando Alegre offers three tiers of employment, to perfectly match your experience and aptitudes." The accented narrator droned on.

Colored graphs appeared, showing how many workers did what. The white section was the smallest group and a green banner across the sparse stick figures indicated *No positions currently available.* Most of the chart was red. More footage of farms and fields, and brown people toiling in them. Scientists in research coats, white people eating in a fancy restaurant, Hispanic women in business suits, cattle, children seated in rows— hands raised with enthusiasm. *Get on with it already!*

"The Blue Tier is for maintenance and skilled labor. All other participants will report to Red Tier: farming and livestock. All participants will receive housing, a generous base salary, and health benefits. Those who qualify will ascend to the White Tier. This is for researchers, educators, and management. These positions offer the best pay and benefits."

Of course they do. They're not hiring!

"...and require strict confidentiality agreements and restrictive residency." Restrictive residency? What did that even mean?

Whatever it was, I had to do it. What choice did I have?

Julia was all smiles when I gave her my forms. She told me they'd send a van for me tomorrow with everything I'd need for orientation. I gave them Tito's address. If I was accepted, and Julia made it sound like I would be; there'd be a physical, and then I'd be offered a contract for one tier or another.

I was almost out the door when a sharp tap on my shoulder made me turn around. Ah yes, the only other college grad from the neighborhood. He was wearing a blue jumper like in the training film. Didn't make the White Tier, I see. Tough luck, man.

"Miguel! What's up man? How's your sis—" he leaned forward and spoke in a harsh whisper. "You got to get out of here. Tito is a liar. Don't believe anything he tells you." Miguel looked around nervously. He'd lost some weight since I'd seen him last. Over Miguel's shoulder, Julia eyed us with interest. "Leave now and don't come back."

"What the hell, man? You can't just tell me to—" Miguel shook his head urgently and started to say something else. I couldn't hear him. An unholy buzzing tore through the air. It was long, loud, a low-pitch version of nails on a chalkboard. Everyone in their blue, red, or white uniforms stopped in unison, turned around and disappeared through various doors. Miguel followed them. Soon the lobby was empty except for me and Julia.

"See you tomorrow!" She intoned cheerfully. Julia leaned forward to reveal cleavage I hadn't noticed before. She smiled and waved like she was Queen of a parade float.

"Miguel told you not to trust me? ¡A' Poco! You know he just wants that White Tier job all to himself!" Tito sounded both drunk and furious as we sat in his garage on my last night of unemployment.

"The movie they showed said there weren't any White Tier jobs open. How'd you know about it anyway?" I helped myself to another beer, dropping a wedge of lime in the bottle before I drank.

"Just because his sister bailed on Trabajando Alegre,

that's no reason for him to be trash talkin'. Everybody needs the money. That's no reason to screw you over, Amigo. You can't listen to that guy, man." I sat on the cot Tito set me up with for the night.

"She left? The sister? Why would she leave?"

"¡Me vale!" His shrug let me know how little he cared about the personal life of Miguel's sister. He took a shot of tequila and poured another for us both.

"Hey, that's enough for me." I told him, wondering how anyone could hold a job and drink so much. "I gotta be up early tomorrow to pretend to be uneducated." Tito laughed and reminded me that getting wasted the night before could only make that easier.

It was the best sleep I'd had in weeks.

A blue and gold *Trabajando Alegre* van pulled up in front of Tito's place five minutes early. I made it to Julia's desk ten minutes ahead of schedule, and gave her a nod. She pointed me to a door where the word 'Interview' appeared, flashed three times, then vanished. I headed in.

"Thank you for coming." There were two executives, a man about forty with ridiculous muttonchops and a woman slightly older with beehive hair. They wore nearly identical black jackets with pale blue shirts underneath. "We'd like to ask you a few questions, and then have you take a few aptitude tests, okay?" The man with muttonchops seemed friendly when he spoke. I nodded while the he shuffled through the forms I filled out yesterday. "It says here that you have a GED. Is that correct?"

"Yes," I lied. Guilt clawed and scratched at my insides. I swallowed.

"Good." The woman spoke now, in the tone Mrs. Bee uses when teenagers disrespect the books. "What was your final GPA?" She asked, looking down.

"Three point four," I told her proudly. Muttonchops closed his eyes, looking embarrassed. Shit. That was a mistake.

"A grade-point average for a GED. Interesting." She wrote something down, still not looking at me. "I was of the understanding that GED testing was pass/fail. Hmmm. Learn something new every day, isn't that right Paolo? May I call you Paolo?" I nodded, feeling a little sick.

"Ma'am, the other candidate should be arriving." Muttonchops said, pouring himself water from a glass jug on the table.

"Water, Paolo?" The woman asked. I nodded again, suddenly drained and dehydrated. I gulped the water in the paper cone, then refilled it twice more as it threatened to collapse in my hand.

The door opened. Miguel. Dammit! He was already sending $1,200 a month to his family. Even half of that would be enough for them to live on. What else could he possibly— Geez. He looked terrified.

"Thank you for coming, Miguel. This is Paolo, the other candidate we'll be considering." Miguel shook my hand, shaking as if he'd never met me before. I stared into him but said nothing. Snake! He's a snake and a liar. I just knew he'd try to snake me out of this job. It was hot in here. Hot.

The clawing in my gut intensified, and I helped myself to another paper cone of water.

"If you don't mind, we'll leave you gentlemen here for a moment to fill out these questionnaires." The man said as both of them stood, buttoned their blazers and exited, leaving me alone with that snake Miguel. His eyes went huge as he turned to me, shaking his head frantically when I started to speak. Yeah, he didn't want to hear it, but he was going to.

"Look Miguel, I don't know what you're trying to pull, or why you think you can snake me out of this job, but—" He knocked the full paper cone of water out of my hand, he was babbling so low and fast I could barely understand him.

"There's a restaurant, behind the building. That's where

they go with those trays. We're... cattle to them. They treat us like—" Miguel whined and whispered, but he wasn't about to put one over on me. I wasn't going anywhere.

I finished the water and debated pouring more. The pitcher was almost empty. The door opened. The beehive woman walked in with two large men in uniforms identical to Miguel's.

"I think that's quite enough talking Mister Managua." She said. The Blue Tier men subdued Miguel in an instant— he didn't even fight them. They strapped him down and rolled him out on a metal dolly like Hannibal the Cannibal in that movie. It was hot in here. The paper cone crumbled like soggy dust in my hand. Weak. Dizzy. My head hit the table hard. Eyes... closed.

Metallic clangs, rhythmic, loud. Moans. Pained gurgling and gulping. Multitudes. A long, shrill scream— female. I was dizzy and unsteady, alarmed to realize I was moving down a sterile white hallway at a good clip. I clenched my eyes shut tight, knowing I didn't want to see whatever inspired the ghoulish cacophony around me. Stench rose up, shit and piss and dead things like the farm near Abuelo's; the family died and no one knew for a month. The men who finally cleaned it up wore hazmat suits.

Wherever they were taking me, it was steeped in misery. How could I work in a place like— but I was kidding myself. This wasn't work. It was... some kind of torture. Sound around me suddenly stopped. We passed through whatever it was and into someplace bright. Water. Cold. Drenched. Freezing. Lavender. *Lavender?* . Blinding light.

"That's got most of the stink off you. You can open your eyes." A familiar woman's voice said. I did. It was the Beehive lady. Muttonchops stood next to her in front of a huge window revealing a scene of abject horror. Someone rolled me over to it, confirming that I was on a dolly like the one that carried Miguel away.

"Take a nice, long look." Beehive lady said, gesturing

to the unspeakable Red Tier. Farming and livestock. *Live-stock*. ¡Madre de Dios! They leaned my dolly forward, forcing me to behold the horrors below.

Perhaps two-dozen heavyset brown-skinned men and women bound by what looked like a thick, plastic casing. They stood in rows, arms pinned to flank, legs tied together, heads forced back so their eyes faced almost directly up. Tubes ran down their throats from somewhere above. They shook and gagged, but were bound too tightly to escape.

"Those who are out of shape for real work are sent here, where their fatty organs can do the most good for our sponsors." Beehive lady said with cold cruelty. "Have you ever had foie gras? Of course you haven't. It costs a week's wage for someone like you." She chuckled merrily and whoever was pushing my dolly sniggered. "Perhaps you've had veal? The tender young flesh is just ...."

The back of my throat went acidic as I felt vomit rising up, wanting out. Across the blood soaked room were wooden stalls the size of dog carriers. Young women down on all fours, boxed in and shackled. Oversize baby bottles hung in front of their faces, containing a beige liquid none of them were drinking. A man in a red jumper paced before the bound women, spraying each with a large hose that made them struggle helplessly in their chains and boxes.

"Your friend Mister Managua thought he'd be clever, that he'd warn people, keep them away. He's getting the full *Kobe* treatment now." She gestured to the window, and a light went on in the far corner. Miguel, strapped to a hospital gurney, struggled feebly as two men rubbed his legs with a shiny oil. His back was tiger-striped with bright red welts. These bastards had taken a whip to him! "They'll keep him like that for a few months. He'll eat well, until it's his time to feed others." Months? My God. If people found out about this....

We turned the corner that revealed another long window, and a kind of conveyor belt whirring by. I was reminded of a scary bedtime story Abuela used to tell me, about villagers who sought out *Long Pig* in the winter when food was scarce. When I was fifteen she finally told me that *long pig* was people. I thought it was just a story. Seeing the emptied torsos moving mechanically down the conveyor, I was struck by how much they looked like stock footage of beef and pork processing plants. We *are* mammals... made of meat.

This was the United States of America— the country that proclaimed more than any other to be the 'greatest nation on earth,' while its citizens were being butchered to feed the rich. That fancy pants restaurant, for their 'sponsors.' People would find out about this. A horror of this magnitude couldn't go on forever. Someone would talk. Someone must have a conscience. Looking around, I couldn't see anyone who betrayed even a whisper of morality. Beehive lady and Muttonchops were as dead inside as I would likely be soon. Best case scenario, they'd let me process my own people into cannibal delicacies; worst, I'd be slowly tortured into someone's dinner.

Bodies went by in front of me. Gutted, empty inside. Large figures dressed head-to-toe in red, removed arms and legs from the hanging meat— wait— *people*. Dammit, they weren't meat, they were people. MY people.

"This doesn't have to be your fate," Beehive lady said. "You're intelligent, educated, looking toward being a family man. We can make you a Company Man. We've got them on the outside. If you think for a moment, you'll realize that you know at least one of our people already."

Tito. Shit! Anger mixed with fear in my gut, my chest, I trembled so hard I thought my straps had come loose Hulk-style. I could kill that bastard.

They removed my leg straps and let me stand, though my arms remained pinned to my sides. My hands moved like flippers.

"We require a fixed amount of new product every month," Muttonchops said like he was explaining something to a child. "You begin by finding a suitable replacement for yourself, your weight or heavier. Then you just have to find us one new applicant each year— we will allow you to remain on the outside without joining any of the usual tiers."

Applicants, he called them. Applicants to be chopped up into fancy dinner for snobby rich assholes? It was obscene, unthinkable, madness. He went on to explain that they also get 'livestock' from prisons, hospitals, some were even purchased from family members to forgive debts.

A replacement for myself? Could I possibly trick someone into... this? What kind of man would that make me? How would I live with myself if I knowingly... who could possibly deserve something so.... Like a punch in both eyes at once— it hit me. I *did* know someone who deserved, who *needed* to be taken out of decent society and brought here, used for this. He'd do more good here than he'd ever do on the outside. I nodded to the devils in blazers.

"Very good." Muttonchops smiled and looked to Beehive lady, who nodded. My straps loosened and the attitude of everyone in the room completely changed. Muttonchops clapped me on the back as if we were fraternity brothers. We walked together down another blinding-white hallway, and onto an elevator that opened into a fancy dining room. "There is one caveat, Paolo," he said, and I wished I'd never told him to call me by my first name, "We will know if you divulge our secrets to anyone. Is that clear? The Managua girl tested us. She could have been free, instead of foie gras. Shame, really. Pretty girl."

We sat at oak dining tables with lush padded seats. The governor was here, and that white-trash musician who always mouthed off about politics. Trying not to betray my true feelings, I suppressed a gag when I saw Tito at the next table. He sat with two people in identical blazers to Beehive lady and Muttonchops, looming over a plate piled high with meat and potatoes. He was eating... I couldn't even think of it. Without ordering or even menus, Latino wait staff brought us plates heaping with various cuts of meat, and mashed potatoes liberally topped with butter and black truffles. I was so hungry. My last real meal took place when I still had a house to live in.

"Eat up!" Beehive lady shook her fork in my direction, looking from my untouched plate to me. I couldn't. Of course I couldn't touch any of it. Even the roll that sat on a separate plate felt like... I don't know what. Words eluded me, the terror, the nausea, the unstoppable pounding in my head, echoes of the moans, screaming, buzzing saws of that hideous, unholy room.

"Eat!" Beehive lady commanded, snapping me back to where I was. Muttonchops held a hand up to her.

"He doesn't have to. Not yet. It's his first day; let's cut him a break." He thought he was being funny and merciful as he hinted that I'd have to come here again and again. Eventually, they would make me eat. I wrote a name and address on my napkin and asked to leave. Beehive lady looked affronted.

"It doesn't quite work that way," Muttonchops laughed slightly. We'll confirm the address and details of this 'Ernesto,' and when our Blue Tier men have safely subdued him, you can be on your way. You'll be due back here for a progress report 28 days from then."

Screw that. As soon as they let me out of here, I was snatching up Cara and Felix from Ernie's and getting them the hell out of the country. Canada— hell, even Mexico would be better. Soon, soon I'd be free— we all would. And that sonofabitch Ernie would be exactly where he belonged.

I hadn't eaten. I couldn't sleep. It was— like the trite expression, the longest night of my life. Nine hours of weeping, shaking, waiting. Finally. The Blue Tier men called in from Ernie's. It was settled.

A blue and gold *Trabajando Alegre* van, dropped me at Tito's where I'd left my Escort. It was a short drive to pick up Cara and Felix at Ernie's. And he'd be gone. Finally, mercifully gone.

Another familiar blue and gold *Trabajando Alegre* van was pulling out of the drive when I turned the corner onto Ernie's block. They were taking him. It was, like they said, settled. Off to spend the rest of his rotten life on the receiving end of the torture and punishment he's been dishing out all his life.

"Cara? Felix!" I called as I opened the door without knocking. My heart pounded, my breath came fast. "Hey? It's Uncle Paolo. Felix, are you guys awake?" Footsteps, slow and lumbering. I gasped, despite myself.

"Where are they?" He walked out of the kitchen, beer in hand before noon on a Thursday.

"You didn't think I'd let them take ME did you?" Ernie said in a tone colder than even the Beehive lady. "Cara told me you'd come; screamed it at me when they were dragging her and the brat away. I didn't think you'd have the cojones, man." He leveled a gun at me, one I recognized as Tito's. My eyes burned and watered. Tears. It was all for nothing— no. Worse than nothing. Cara and Felix in their green spotted frog hats burned into my brain. I doomed them both. The last words I heard were that bastard, Ernie's.

"Only pussyboys cry! Didn't your Papa ever tell—"

Darkness.

THINGS THEY TOOK FROM LUKE

By

Garrett Cook

Luke's was a good place for a man to get a beer. It was a place for cops, construction workers, plumbers, gravediggers, amateur wrestlers, high school football coaches, car mechanics and loveable welfare slobs. Luke's was the place where all the teenagers knew their dads went to drink and, when they turned twenty-one, were they not the kind of people who left Pig-in-Shit (as in 'happy as a'), Pennsylvania, they would come to Luke's to have beers with their dads. Hell of a place Luke's, where the worst transgressions came down to sex-starved, middle-aged, zombified man-hunting no-man's-brides who didn't care one way or another whether a fella was taken and knew there were no bonds that couldn't be shattered by performing the acts that most men's wives had too damn much integrity to perform. This was the worst thing about Luke's, so Luke's wasn't bad at all.

When you walked into Luke's a chorus of patrons would shout out an enthused greeting. It began with 'hey' and then whatever your name happened to be. If your name was 'Rimjob O' Connor', they would shout out 'hey, Rimjob' or 'hey, Rimmy' or whatever you chose to go by. Sometimes a guy who you knew from work or softball or jail would buy you a drink and it wouldn't be because he was gay and trying to pick you up. There weren't really gays in Pig-in-Shit but if there had been, it would have been okay, because nobody was stupid or a racist like those guys in Satisfied who ran a kid over with their truck just for wearing a Queen t-shirt and then violated his corpse. People in Satisfied were stupid that way, which is why Pig-in-Shit kept on kicking their ass in football. If you were gay and you walked into Luke's somebody would probably buy you a drink without a queer joke, 'cause Luke's was just that kind of place.

"To each his own," Luke always said, because his father had always said "don't stick your nose into nothing that looks like it'll stink too bad." That was advice you could take to the bank. He could've called wives, but that would just wreck families and he could have told husbands to cut it out, but they would have just found somewhere worse to drink at, somewhere where the dregs were twice as low and twice as awful. He never let that happen, so on account of that, people liked Luke.

For the most part, Luke's wife Eileen was happy, but there was something of a dark streak in her, one that wanted to be at the bottom of something scary. The fact that he heard so much good gossip and had so much potential to taste the darker side of human nature, yet never shared any of it with her was even worse than how he never discussed his feelings or how he was almost religiously against going on vacation anywhere. If he shared a drop of his cauldron of bartender's secrets, instead of acting like he was some kind of goddamn doctor who swore confidentiality, then she would have been that much happier and the seed of rebellion wouldn't have been planted. Things could have been perfect.

Then again, they probably couldn't have. Everything started to go south for Luke. If he had to pinpoint the moment, it was when Bob White, came in and bought rounds for everybody. While most of the time Bob White was not particularly happy about bein' an undertaker, tonight he was dancing on air. As everybody raised their glasses for him, he burst out laughing. He almost fell off his stool. It was only polite to ask just what was so funny. In the future, when he looked back at this moment, Luke would feel even sadder than usual, because that laughter was a herald of the huge fucking mess that was to come, the mess that ate Pig-in-Shit.

"You wouldn't believe the day I had," said Bob White, still unable to stop laughing, "this hot little city chick shows up in black lingerie and some kind of weird Kiss makeup and she's carrying a great big briefcase...."

"What'd she have in the briefcase? You need to bury a dwarf?" Hank Browning asked him. It was hard to tell whether Hank was joking or actually intrigued by the possibility that someone could carry a dead dwarf in a big old briefcase.

"No, Hank, the briefcase did not have a dwarf in it. It might have been a big one, but dwarfs don't come that small. She came in and she asked me, 'you Bob White, the undertaker?' 'That's what the sign says,' I say. 'I need two dozen coffins,' she says. 'I don't have time for jokes,' I say. 'I don't either, Mr. White,' she says real sexy. She opens up the briefcase, and it's full of stacks of hundred dollar bills. It takes me two hours to do all the math and the counting, but I work it all out, count out every dime of that money and damned if she did not have enough money on her to buy two dozen coffins!"

"Shit, Bob," said Luke, "that's a good day of business."

"Sure is." Bob replied. He still couldn't stop laughing.

Next day it was Hank Browning and the boys from his construction company that strolled in triumphant.

"Damnedest thing happened to me today, Luke. Biggest job I've ever gotten. Lots of money up front. Would you believe a castle, Luke?"

"Congratulations, Hank."

This served as a cue for Hank's friendly rival Victory Sampson and his crew to show up. They ordered drinks for the whole bar too. They all sat down and laughed at their good fortune.

"Luke, my friend, business is good all-around in Pig-in-Shit," said Victory. "Today my boys got commissioned for a castle, a real fortress in the hills. Don't that beat all, old friend?"

"Rich folk have funny tastes, Victory. Maybe that Paris Hilton bitch is buildin' herself two castles just to fill 'em up with coffins to store drugs."

"That'd be a lot of drugs."

"Not for somebody who can build two castles."

Retribution Jones stepped into the light. Everybody in the bar shivered a little. They swore the old stinking drunk had decided that God had put him on this earth to make sure people couldn't go about their business without thinking about werewolves, Bigfoot and cursed summer camps. If there was a moment Retribution could not render weird or awkward, they hadn't found it yet.

"Luke, it ain't like that. You should know by now to ask yourself questions when things like this come up and not to just trust everybody out there. Ain't gonna survive livin' like that. Think for a moment, who needs castles and coffins? Who has the money to do whatever they please? Ain't no Paris Hilton drug den comin' here, no sir. It's the undead. Dracula, Nosferatu, all those dead bloodsuckin' types. They know it's not right around here. The devil's had his eye on these parts. He's gonna get it all, just you wait and see, you poor naïve sons-of-bitches!"

The awkward silence was shattered when Wilhelmina Fencepost, the realtor came in full of piss and vinegar and bought drinks for the entire bar. Business had obviously been good for her that day, too since somebody had to buy land to put those two castles on.

"My god, Luke, you would not believe the good fortune that's come to Pig-in-Shit. I'm sure the construction boys have told ya about the castles, but there's even more than that!"

"Wilhelmina, I'm not surprised."

"Buyin' up a bunch of farmland at the edge of town and

the land where the old paint factory used to stand. The whole damn town should celebrate, Luke. Farming's come back and with it plenty of jobs."

Retribution dropped to the floor and began to weep. "Why don't you listen? The undead are coming! Vampires! Bloodsuckers! Monsters! They're gonna eat us! We're all doomed!"

Off-duty cop Harry Castle resigned himself to once more dragging Retribution to the drunk tank. They should've been suspicious of this particular outburst, should have thought about how crazy men know certain things that sane ones don't. Not a sane man in Luke's could have expected any of the events that were to fall upon Pig-in-Shit. Not a sane man in Luke's could even have expected the lovely pale Goth chick that came in soon after Retribution was dragged from the premises.

"You must be cold," Luke said, eyeing her scantily clad form. Any woman clad in nothing but tattoos, a thong and a black bustier was out of place.

"I'll have a Cosmopolitan." Time stopped as she ordered.

"This is a bar, not a newsstand," Luke said.

"Did I say something, wrong?"

"We don't really make mixed drinks around here."

"I will have a rum and coke, I suppose. You do know how to make a rum and coke, Luke?"

"I've got Bacardi."

She winced. "Bacardi will have to do."

She tipped Luke a twenty and that was enough to make him understand.

As castles went up and shops were bought out and closed down, more Goth chicks came into Luke's for Cosmopolitans and other fruity drinks. As a wolfish cloud came down upon the sun, a fanged biker gang stirred up trouble with the locals, which Luke sat and watched. The citizenry began to farm turnips for their livelihood, these ruffians began to come in more often, trashing the bar and then using big fat vampire checks to make it all better. Pig-in-Shit and Luke did better than ever. He thought about ignoring his convictions and taking his wife on a trip around the world, but he didn't because the vampire ruffians might do something drastic if he wasn't there to harass when they felt like harassing somebody.

The leader of these ruffians was Hamilton. Though the sun was long gone, he was never seen without shades. He dressed like a biker, but his gang consisted of a Renaissance Harlequin, a Confederate General, three plaid shirted redneck shit-kickers and an English punk whose bleach blonde Mohawk featured prominent pink streaks. First time they came in, Luke was stupid enough to call the cops. After the blood was mopped up nobody called the cops again. Luke's became a place where vampire thugs had loud, sloppy sex with Goth groupies on every table, then smashed the jukebox. Luke's became a personal hell for Luke.

Being married to Luke became a personal hell for Eileen. He went from inexpressive to outright crabby. He didn't touch her, and he complained about those damn kids and their weird clothes and their vandalism and their, their... mmm. It became clear to Eileen she could be leading a much more stimulating life, so one day she came into Luke's in full white face makeup, a red teddy she hadn't worn since her honeymoon, and a pair of four-inch heels she had bought years ago in case she wanted an affair. Right in front of Luke, on one of Luke's own tables, Eileen became Hamilton's new old lady.

As anybody could expect, this was the final straw. Luke had gone from disliking vampires to hating vampires. He had to think of a clever way to be rid of them.

Father Conroy's church had been shut down, but he was still ordained and therefore in a position to bless things. As a raging alcoholic, he was more than willing to bless all of Luke's beer in exchange for a keg.

As expected, Hamilton ordered extremely manly

quantity of beer. As expected, Hamilton chugged it really fast. As expected, Hamilton went up in flames and was shocked enough by divinity poisoning that Luke had the opportunity to shove a broken chair leg stake into his heart. Body flaming from heavenly retribution, stake in heart, the vampire crumbled into ashes. The remainder of the gang fled in terror, although Eileen did stop to shoot her husband a glare and ask "Why won't you let me be happy?"

Sporting a monocle and a gigantic stovepipe hat and accompanied by six chainsaw wielding Goth chick minions, former undertaker and newly elected Burgomeister Bob White forced his way into Luke's house, dragging the man from bed as he read from an invisible list of charges.

"By my authority as Burgomeister, I hereby arrest you, Luke Vespucci for the crimes of necrocide, utilizing weaponized Christianity, poisoning a patron of your bar and interrupting vampiric shenanigans. How do you plead?"

"You're already dragging me from my house. Why do I need to plead?"

"Point is, don't do the crime if you can't do the time. So confess," Bob White said.

"Okay, I confess."

"Thanks for makin' this easy, Luke."

"Well, you're a friend, Bob."

Before he knew it, Luke was manacled to the wall in a dank, medieval dungeon. He was amazed something built this recently could look so spooky. In spite of his appreciation for the craftsmanship, he was perturbed by the cackling, ominous shadows and skeletons that danced outside his cell for hours. He knew these things were designed to put him in a state of mortal terror, but for him they were simply nuisances. The vampires had a way of missing how scary life could be without the trappings of terror. He almost pitied them.

On the third night of Luke's captivity, he dreamt of Eileen. She was made of hot dogs and wild dingoes tore her arms off. Luke tried to shoo them away.

"Don't bother the dingoes, Luke," Eileen sobbed.

"What do you mean? They're eatin' you!"

"Don't bother the dingoes. This is what I like to do now."

"You like to be eaten by wild dogs?"

Eileen sighed.

"You never listen, Luke."

"You're not making any sense, Eileen."

"That's because you never listen. You never did before, either."

"Eileen, I demand you stop being made out of meat, right this instant! No wife of mine is going to get off on being eaten by dingoes!"

Eileen laughed.

"Too little, too late, Luke. You barely seemed to care as it happened. You can't tell me what to do anymore. Might seem like silly bullshit to you, but it's my life now."

"Eileen, stop this!"

The dingoes pulled the hotdog arms from her sockets and Eileen squealed with glee, squeals which grew into orgasmic moans.

"Chew them, doggies, chew them!"

"Eileen!"

"This is what I like to do!"

Luke's eyes opened to find Hamilton's boys had gathered outside his cell. The Confederate General pointed, laughed and rattled his saber. The harlequin smashed balloon animals in obscene shapes while making stinging barbs in Italian followed by gales of unrestrained laughter. The redneck shit-kickers engaged in a vigorous square dance, which they capped off with fart noises. The mohawked punk engaged in a weird jig that Luke assumed must have been to mock him, but was not certain how. Was the punk saying that Luke was some kind of hayseed? Was he claiming he was stupid?

The mohawked punk pressed his face through the bars of the cell.

"Do you like my dance, sweetheart? Does it turn you on?"

"No."

The punk must have assumed his display was actually getting to Luke, because he kept it up.

"You're old, old man!" the punk said.

"Not as old as we are!" cackled the harlequin. A chorus of directionless laughter erupted from the rest.

"Look, the old man's gonna cry." the mohawked one laughed.

At this point they were right. Luke was close to tears from having the dream that he had and seeing the company his wife now kept. As he attempted to hold back the tears, he bit his tongue. Biting his tongue gave him an idea that brought him some slight satisfaction even in this position. He drew blood and knew that he they noticed. He bit harder and was certain that for them the room was now intolerably full of bloodscent. "Make them suffer," he said to himself "Make them hungry. If you're lucky, Luke, they'll kill ya."

The mohawked one, most demonstrative in general, was the first to lose it.

"We'll eat you, old man!"

"Gonna rip you up!"

"Kill you!"

"Gut you!"

"Smash your old bones! Rip you up!"

When the mohawked one got close enough to bare fangs right in Luke's face, Luke spat a big gob of blood onto the asshole's forehead. The other vampires emitted a series of low growls and their eyes began to glow fire engine red. They skulked towards their bloodstained friend.

"Stop it! Stop it, you animals! We're going to kill the old bastard, remember?" the mohawked one screeched.

"Then do it!" Luke shouted.

Once he did, he realized he shouldn't have done that. The sadists left and let him be. It was to Luke's credit that it wasn't until then that he cried, for his town, for his old life, for his wife, for all the things that they had taken from him. The last thing he had, his dignity was gone as well.

Don't survive this, Luke, whatever you do, don't survive this.

It was right at this moment when the girl entered. She looked about nineteen years old, must have weighed ninety pounds sopping wet as Luke could see bits of ribcage underneath her Bob Marley t-shirt. Her dreads were as out of place as she would have been in Pig-in-Shit a few months back and had the texture of bundled straw.

Luke yawned. "Are you going to kill me?"

"Nope," the skinny pseudohippy replied, "but I'm gonna slap you."

She did and it might have taken Luke's head off if it were much harder.

"Look, dude, I'm sorry, I don't go in for the whole like violent warpig hittin' thing, but you're one miserable motherfucker."

"Let me die...."

She reached into her all hemp handbag and pulled out a joint.

"No can fucking do. You killed Hamilton. Takes balls. I'm gonna need somebody with balls."

"What if they catch me again?"

"They won't. I explained to those geniuses that they can't trash you're bar when you're not there to run it. You're in business forever, dude, 'til the plan works, that is."

"Why are you doing this?"

She lit the joint and inhaled deep.

"To piss off my dad."

With the blessing of the young vampiress, Luke the bartender made his escape. And the rich fops that had absorbed the town he had loved so much would see what it was to face a man they could take nothing more from.

THE RULES

By

Lizz-Ayn Shaarawi

Eddie raced in the house, slamming the front door behind him. He set the alarm and stumbled back, nearly falling over the easy chair he'd inherited from his father. Allowing himself to sink into the plush cushions, he thought back to his pop and how disappointed he would be right now. Eddie had managed to break every one of his father's rules in one job.

Rule one: Make sure the house is empty.

The old man was supposed to be off at his weekly poker game. Eddie cased the house for weeks and the mark, old jeweler that lived alone in a huge house that doubled as his studio, was like clockwork. He only went out for groceries and the poker game. But not this night, the one night Eddie needed him gone, he'd come back for his wallet and caught Eddie red handed.

Rule Two: Never let a mark see your face.

When Eddie rounded the corner of the living room, he met the old man face-to-face. They both stood statue still for a split second before the old man charged him, cane raised.

Rule Three: No one gets hurt.

It was self-defense, really. He never wanted to hurt the old man. Old bones are brittle and snap so easily. Eddie should have bolted right then but that's when he saw the necklace.

Rule Four: Only take what's on the list.

The necklace looked ancient. Delicate twists of gold and silver surrounded what looked like old coins but they weren't from any country Eddie recognized. It seemed to call to him. His fingers closed around the necklace before he'd even realized he'd done it.

The old man spoke in a strange accent. "Not the necklace. She's the only thing I care about. Please."

It was too late. That necklace suddenly became the one thing Eddie wanted in the entire world. If he wasn't positive he'd end up fish food in the East River, he'd have dropped the rest of the goods and just taken the necklace. But Big Louie was not a person who took disappointment well and Eddie had enough sense of self-preservation to hang on to the bag.

The old man cried as Eddie stepped over him and he clung to Eddie's leg. "Please. Don't take it. Anything but that."

Eddie shook his leg loose and kept walking.

Jesus, his Pop would smack him if he were here right now. Eddie hauled himself out of the chair and into the kitchen. Bright light bounced off of sterile countertops. Eddie stashed the necklace in the freezer. He opened the fridge and grabbed a can of beer. Opening it over the sink, he slurped up the foam as it spilled over the top.

A knock at the door made him jump, spilling his beer. He cursed and rushed over to the big screen T.V. to turn it on. Security cameras showed various views throughout the house and grounds. One picture depicted a very large man standing on the front step giving the camera the finger.

Eddie punched in the security code. A series of beeps and the front door opened.

"Louie."

"Eddie."

They stared at each other with poker faces. "You here for a pick up?" Eddie asked.

Louie pushed past Eddie and made himself comfortable

on the sofa. "I heard you had a problem at the jewelers."

Eddie shrugged. "He wasn't supposed to be home."

Louie shook his head. "Bad for business, man." The large man leaned back and rested his ample arm across the back of the sofa. "Lucky for you, by the time his poker buddies realized something was wrong and called the paramedics, he was 'unresponsive.'" Louie made air quotes with his sausage-like fingers.

"Yeah, lucky me." Eddie took a swig of the beer.

Louie stared at him.

Eddie stared back. "What? You want a beer?"

"You got reduced calorie?"

"Beer? Hell no!"

Louie frowned. "I'm watching my weight these days."

"Good for you."

"Don't get smart."

"I'm not, honest."

Louie shifted in his seat. "We've worked together a long time, Eddie. And your pop worked for my pop."

"Where you going with this?"

"The jeweler don't make it, we're good. But if he comes to...." Louie left it hanging. He didn't have to say. Eddie already knew.

Eddie tossed the bag of stolen goods over to Louie who caught it with surprising ease. "Thanks for the house call, Louie."

Louie grunted and puffed as he tried to stand. Eddie held out a hand, but Louie slapped it away. With quite a bit of rocking, he managed to hoist himself from the sofa and waddle to the door. He held up the bag in farewell. "For the record, I'm rooting for you."

Eddie smirked. "You're warming the cockles of my heart."

"Yeah, I got your cockles right here." Louie laughed, which turned into a wheezing cough, and headed out the door. Eddie locked it behind him.

"Fat bastard."

He set the alarm and poured the rest of his beer down the sink.

~

Eddie slept fitfully. He kicked his covers off and moaned. A shadow passed by his bed and paused near his head. Darkness fell across his face. His breathing stopped.

The shadow moved away.

Eddie bolted upright in bed and gasped for air. His gaze darted around the empty room. A car drove by, its headlights throwing more shadows across the wall. Eddie winced against the light and tossed his covers aside. A quick glance at the clock showed it was just past midnight.

Trudging down the stairs, Eddie yawned and wiped his eyes. He caught a glimpse of movement from the kitchen. Dropping to a crouch, he half-crawled to a baseboard near the bottom of the stairs. He popped the wood open, revealing a hiding spot. A small handgun and ammunition occupied the narrow space.

Eddie checked to make sure the gun was loaded and clicked the safety off.

Why wasn't the alarm shrieking? Did he forget to set it? Doesn't matter now, he supposed.

Shadows shifted again as Eddie crept towards the kitchen. Gun raised, he hazarded a glance around the divider wall and stopped dead in his tracks.

A gorgeous naked woman stood in front of his refrigerator. No, not naked. She wore a strange semi-sheer flesh colored dress that clung to her curves. Long copper curls cascaded down her back. The stolen necklace draped across her long, pale throat.

Any other time, Eddie would have been interested in getting to know her better. Under the circumstances, all he wanted to know was why she was there, and how he was going to get that necklace the hell off of her.

Eddie opened his mouth to speak.

She startled him when she spoke first. "You do not have a lot of food." She spoke in the same strange accent as the jeweler.

"I wasn't expecting company," Eddie said.

"It is good to be prepared." She studied the contents of a take-out container.

Eddie flashed the gun. "I like to think I do okay."

She tossed the container back into the fridge as turned to face him and he felt as if he'd just gotten kicked in the gut. God, she was beautiful. The bronze ringlets bounced of their own accord as she swiveled around. He aimed the pistol at her.

She laughed and strode over to him. Her hand slid over his as she lower the gun, pointing the barrel at the floor. The touch felt electric.

"You're trespassing," Eddie whispered.

She leaned close to his ear. Her breath tickled the hair on his neck. "You going to shoot me with your... gun?"

"If I have to," Eddie said.

"Why you shoot me? I do nothing wrong." Her lips brushed his neck.

He swallowed hard and it made a clicking sound in his dry throat.

"I don't appreciate someone waltzing in here and trying to take what I rightfully stole."

She laughed and it sounded like rain on a tin roof. "This is my necklace. Naughty boy."

"Take it off." Eddie demanded.

"No." Her eyes twinkled with mischief.

He raised the gun and again she gently lowered it. "I trade you for it?" She purred.

She leaned in, her mouth centimeters from his.

He could feel her heat. "What kind of trade?"

"Anything you want."

He smiled. "Anything?"

He grabbed a handful of those copper tresses and

pulled her head back. She laughed again and nodded. "Anything."

Eddie's eyes traveled over her body. The dress didn't leave much to the imagination.

She smiled to see his hunger. "So you tell me what you want."

He pulled her close and murmured into her ear. "I want you to take off that necklace and get the hell out of my house." He pushed her away.

Her face twisted into a snarl. "I try to go the easy way but you do not play. So now we go the hard way."

It was Eddie's turn to laugh. "Bring it, honey."

The muscles under her skin rippled. Two horned bumps rose from her forehead. Her shoulders expanded and claws sprouted from her fingertips.

Eddie's hands trembled as he aimed the gun and fired. The woman's body jerked back with the impact but the bullet failed to even faze her. She advanced.

Eddie fired twice more with the same result. She growled and charged him. He turned, and dashed out of the room.

As he fled through the living room, he accidentally stepped on the remote control. The television powered on. The screen showed the security feeds. Eddie raced over to the alarm panel by the front door and hit the panic button. A siren blared.

Eddie scanned the room. She was gone. He glanced over at the security feed. It showed room after empty room.

He was alone.

"Jesus. I must be losing my mind." he whispered to himself.

A shadow rose up behind him. He whirled around as the woman loomed over him. She lunged.

He ducked and slid across the hardwood floor just out of her grasp.

She snarled as she gave chase.

He took the stairs two at a time.

She stormed up after him.

He dove into the master bedroom and barred the door behind him. A low growl issued from the other side. The door burst open as Eddie dove behind the bed. The woman grabbed Eddie by the ankle and dragged him out.

He clawed the floor.

She flipped him onto his back and straddled him. Strong fingers forced Eddie's mouth open.

He fought and twisted but her muscular legs pinned him to the floor. She placed her open mouth over his. Their eyes locked as she inhaled.

As she pulled the life force from Eddie's body, they both shrank. She returned to her small, beautiful female form. He collapsed inward, practically deflated, and became an empty shell. His lifeless eyes rolled back and stared at the ceiling. She climbed off his body and wiped the back of her mouth.

Her fingers played across the delicate necklace. "I give this back to my master now, yes?"

She nudged the corpse with her toe. "I take your silence as agreement."

The front door splintered inward as the police responded to the alarm. They darted from room to room, shouting "Clear!" as they went.

When the first policeman, the rookie, entered the bedroom, he fainted. The second policeman, Officer Murphy, had to put his head between his knees to keep from vomiting. When Officer Diaz, arrived, he stepped over the first and past the second, leaned down to peer at Eddie's desiccated corpse. "Well, that ain't something you see every day."

Murphy managed to find his voice. "It's one of Big Louie's boys. What the hell did they do to him?"

Diaz shook his head. "No idea, but I hope I never cross whoever did it."

A glint of metal caught Murphy's eye. Leaning in for a closer look, he spotted the necklace. An uncontrollable urge overtook him and he lunged for the jewelry. Diaz grabbed his shoulder and pulled him back.

"What the hell's wrong with you? You know the rules! Don't touch anything until forensics gets here."

Murphy's face reddened. "Sorry. I don't know what came over me." His gaze drifted back to the necklace.

Diaz crouched over Eddie's body. "How do you think they made him shrink like that?"

Murphy took the opportunity to snatch the bauble. He shoved it deep in his pocket. "No idea, man. I wouldn't get to close, though."

Diaz nodded. "You're right." Diaz stepped back. "That shit might be contagious." Murphy nodded, only half hearing his partner as his hand stole back to the necklace in his pocket.

THE SECOND VAULT

By

Andrew G. Dombalagian

Horatio coughed another mouthful of foul water from his lungs onto the pebbly beach. With each wracking convulsion, his fingers gouged furrows in the sand. His gilded pocket watch swung in slow arcs from the brass chain coiled around the slim fingers of the woman who dragged him from the water. Horatio caught fleeting, blurred images of her through the darkness of Lake Michigan. When he could trust his eyes again, he saw that her off-white gown was bone dry, although its edges were frayed and tattered with ominous ruddy patches on the fabric. Her loose hair was the color of deep earth; her eyes were a piercing silver that gleamed from the shadows lining her sharp face.

The fading night passed in silence as Horatio recovered from his near-death experience, and his strange rescuer sat enthroned upon a splintered log washed onto the shore. She eyed him like a child watching a curious bug crawl along the Earth.

Who're you?" Horatio finally croaked the question.

His companion mulled her answer, or she simply ignored the question for a few final moments. "Call me Elizabeth."

"Why'd you pull me from the water?"

"It is not your time to die. It is rather presumptuous of you to usurp the Fates' duty for yourself. There is still much left for you to accomplish."

If his mind were not so muddled, Horatio may have found this woman's own presumption to be infuriating. Instead, he merely felt baffled. Of all the questions clambering to the forefront of his water-logged mind, it was her keen interest in his pocket watch that surfaced first.

"Why're you so interested in that damnable watch?"

"I have never seen anything quite like it."

"You can have it. I couldn't even pawn it to buy a meal. It's phony. Cheap copper on wood."

Bored by the watch, Elizabeth eyed the tiny flecks of light running along the lakeside and into the distance. The pair sat on a dark, deserted stretch of beach. The remnants of a rumrunner's boat, smashed apart by treasury agents many months ago, lay scattered and rotting like a broken beast's ribcage.

"There are so many other hopeless individuals in this city."

"Welcome to Chicago. The G-Men may have given back all the hooch, but that don't mean anything's improved. Still ain't no jobs, ain't no money. Heck, I miss the gangsters. Before they put Capone away, at least a fella could count on his generosity at a bread line."

Elizabeth turned her narrowing eyes to Horatio. A grin's ghost flashed across her face.

"How fortunate that you mention that name. Instead of a handout, would you accept an opportunity? There are many hopeless people in this city, but none who will ever see a glimmer of hope like I can offer you."

"What're you going on about, dame?" Horatio spat the question out with the last of the lake water from his gullet.

"Follow me and find out." Elizabeth climbed the sandy hill away from the beach and slipped into the park trees.

Horatio swept the sand from his sodden clothes. He rose and took the first of many heavy steps after Elizabeth.

~

Horatio A. Lerge begrudgingly introduced himself to Elizabeth, his reviled savior who shared the name with his long dead grandmother. He followed her to a boarded up soup kitchen, one among several empty buildings in a bleak row. It would be hours until the first glimmers of morning light peered through the brown haze over the city, so the darkness cloaked them when Elizabeth pried the wooden slats off the dingy door with her bare hands. Through the darkness inside, she found a kerosene lamp which she lit, even though Horatio could not remember seeing her draw or strike a match.

"I can still hear echoes of the many hungry, tired people who thronged this place: begging, hoping."

Horatio sat on a wormy wooden bench.

"Did you bring me here to mock me about meals I'll never have?"

"Not at all. This is where I make my proposal. I believe you would call it a 'pitch.' What I offer is wealth surpassing your dreams' farthest horizons. You can have money enough to accomplish anything. Will you seize this opportunity to do and become whatever you have always desired?"

"Sounds like some sorta devil's bargain."

"How tragic: you are so cynical that you would spit in the face of hope and fortune? Perhaps I should have left you in the lake and found someone else to profit instead."

"Say I'm interested, what's the scheme? Knock over some banks? Fake some greenbacks? Or are you just going to magically conjure some bread?"

"There is a tunnel under this building. It leads to a series of rooms and halls carved out beneath the city streets. At their heart lies a stronghold: a vault which protects the untold treasures of the deposed street king."

Horatio nearly fell from his bench, aghast at the truth

of Elizabeth's plan.

"We're going to pinch Capone's stash? That's the scheme? Heck, if we try that, I'll end up back in the lake anyhow. It ain't possible!"

"With my help, it will be simple. I know certain things that will ensure our success. If we work together, great things will come about."

"Do I get any time to think it over? Sleep on it?"

"There is no time to spare besides you would not need it anyhow. Your mind is in tumult, but your heart has already decided."

As she turned to slip into the back of the building, Horatio followed Elizabeth. She carried the queerly glowing lamp, but it was the flickering flames of fortunes promised that drew Horatio like a moth. She lured him into the kitchen. Cobwebs shrouded the corpulent black iron stoves, cracking wooden racks, and dusty floors. The last visitors left with every utensil and half-palatable morsel in the place.

Elizabeth stood before the monolithic door of a meat locker. A chain and cumbersome locked sealed it shut. In the dim light, Horatio saw that the chain flaked with rust. When Elizabeth touched the chain, it collapsed into a heap of broken links and cascading dust. She dragged away an empty crate to reveal a trap door in the far corner of the locker. Before she could grasp the iron rung, Horatio had already lifted the hatch open to reveal the ladder descending to the tunnel.

~

The tunnel carried them in shadowy silence for the length of several blocks. Horatio observed the direction and distance they travelled, and from his knowledge of the neighborhood, he grew suspicious.

"What the deuce? Where're we heading?"

"I already told you our destination."

"Yeah, Capone's vault. Capone operated out of the Lexington Hotel. Wouldn't he stash his loot under there? Why're we heading in the opposite direction?"

"More than daring is needed to raid our target. It requires cunning and foreknowledge, and that is why you are fortunate to have my guidance. Yes, as some suspect, Capone hid his bountiful cache beneath the so-called seat of his power. Before he was incarcerated, however, he moved his valuables to a new stronghold. That is where we are heading."

"How do you know about all this? Capone obviously didn't broadcast this switcheroo."

"You are quite right. Aside from two trusted lieutenants, every other crony who knew of the transfer was executed to preserve the secret. Nevertheless, I have access to a font of knowledge which many would kill for, and that is how I have learned of this second hidden vault. I can see you still have questions, but they must wait. I fear that Capone's trust in his surviving underlings was misplaced. Others may be pursuing our goal. We must proceed quietly."

The passage ran straight and narrow, piercing into the city's unknown depths where the hardest men in the country plotted their dirty business. Horatio's already taxed nerves were further jangled by the notion that other fortune-hungry gangsters haunted those tunnels. Horatio had questions deforming into doubt and fear, but there was a barrier in his head preventing him from turning the ideas into words. He might have fled if it hadn't meant receding back into the darkness. The lamp Elizabeth carried was his only light, so a greater fear compelled Horatio to stay with her.

Despite the realization, hesitation slowed his steps like they were caught in molasses. Faint light winked farther down the passage. Elizabeth was leaving him behind in the cold darkness. His arm hairs pricked up. Without warning, the air grew cold and too thick to breathe. An instinct to flail his arms bubbled up from his bowels. Horatio felt like he was drowning in the tunnels. To suppress the upwelling panic, he forced his leaden feet to move and catch up with Elizabeth.

Only seconds had passed, but he somehow lost sight of the enigmatic woman. Entering the weak glow of electric lights nailed to the wooden beams buttressing the walls, Horatio searched through the earthen halls while bringing his panting lungs into line. He passed through several of the rooms Capone and his goons had carved in retreat, connected by these tunnels and shafts.

During Prohibition, the last time Horatio had set foot in a blind pig, it was a dismal scene. He had paid his two bits - money he now mourned - like all the other thirsty patrons to see the morose animals shipped in packing crates while enjoying 'complimentary' cocktails. The gin smelled of industrial ethyl, but it washed down their gullets all the same. The burning refreshment distracted from the drab, torn furnishings, the foul company, and memories of bread lines stretching out into the frost.

The first room Horatio discovered held none of those sullen aspects. It was an abandoned saloon that once served the Chicago gangs in illicit opulence. His fingertips found the seat tops covered in mildewed velvet. The brass fixtures had only just begun to tarnish. Some long lost bootlegger or hired muscle left an overcoat behind in his haste, where Horatio found it undisturbed on its hook. Impressed with its quality, Horatio remembered all that Elizabeth had promised. He removed the coat and slung it over his shoulders: a perfect fit.

Not far from the saloon, Horatio stumbled upon the dusty, claustrophobic remains of another well-appointed room. Narrow divans, couches, plush chairs, and a writing desk cluttered the main room. Horatio poked into a side chamber, discovering a sagging bed, walnut chest of drawers, and an Oriental changing screen embossed with vines and red flower buds. Snooping in the drawers, he discovered a plethora of women's undergarments in the raciest designs of silk, lace, and nylon. With a derisive snort he realized that he had blundered into a bordello: another establishment which, like the saloon, Capone built to slake his men's thirst. Tossing a ball of stockings back into the drawer, Horatio noticed a metallic glint. He fished an unpolished silver cigarette case from the pile of fabrics. He slipped the trinket into the breast pocket of his new overcoat, and for the first time he noticed the monogram on the lapel: H.N.

Exploring the tunnels with a new swagger, Horatio encountered one more room, more spacious and spartan than the others. Rough wooden counters stood in a row like caskets. The room stretched beyond them to a pock-marked earthen wall. The jaundiced light bulbs dangling above cast stark shadows across the bare walls. Stepping up to the counter, Horatio's shoe kicked something that skidded out into the wide space between him and the far wall. A blackened steel revolver shuddered on the stone floor, wobbling away the last of the kick's momentum. As the gun grew still, Horatio understood that it was innumerable bullet holes that riddled the back wall. This was a shooting range. Capone's men stood here and practiced how they would send rivals and lawmen to the county morgue. The cavernous room became oppressively cold, so Horatio fled the emptiness.

He nearly stumbled into Elizabeth, who stood at the top of cut stone stairs leading downward. In a macabre moment, Horatio imagined he could have knocked the woman down into that deeper realm. Her feet never budged an inch; her shoulders and back never shifted from the impact. She may as well have been carved from marble. It dawned on Horatio how silly it was to think a man such as he could move the likes of her, and the thought chilled his spine for an instant.

Elizabeth eyed his new coat with a devilish grin. Despite his vaudevillian bumbling, she seemed pleased with some sort of progress he had made.

"Did you have an enjoyable tour of this secret world? I apologize for not being your guide."

"It ain't no problem. Who'd have thought all this was beneath the streets?"

"I doubt anyone will ever find this place again. While these tunnels were once connected to that other underground stronghold beneath the Lexington, most of those tunnels have been collapsed and erased from history. Soon these walls around us, too, will be sealed away forever. Capone's dying hope for freedom and to return to his horde slips away more and more with every sunset. So much wealth and power all gone to waste."

"Well, we can't let that happen. Let's have at it."

Horatio led the march down the stairs, even though he had no idea where to go or what he must do. Elizabeth kept solemn pace behind him, taking each cement stair with precise, muted grace. The rustle of Horatio's coat could not drown out the rhythmic tapping of metal and stone which echoed from below.

The descent opened into a wide concrete hall supported by a forest of concrete pillars. The blanched walls and supports were bathed in electric yellow light. The metallic tapping was louder and accompanied by an unseen mouth humming a butchered rendition of Toccata & Fugue in D. Three long shadows twisted in disjointed directions across the stone. The silhouettes of curved, hooked arms swung in wide, lethargic arcs in time with the tapping.

Horatio ducked behind a pillar. Elizabeth remained where she stood by the stairs. Horatio's fretful question existed only in his mind, but Elizabeth answered nonetheless. She spoke in a whisper the air carried only to her chosen one's ears. Did Horatio actually see her mouth move to form physical words?

"Although Capone trusted a scant handful of his men with the new location of his treasury, his trust was misplaced. Capone's despair of ever being free translates into tittering ambition for these three men. It fuels the tiresome strokes of their picks and mallets. It will distract them from your approach."

The coat and cigarette case were gifts Horatio gave to himself, but now Elizabeth offered a gift of her own. She revealed a twin of the revolver he had seen in the shooting range. The blackened steel barrel chilled his hand when Elizabeth pressed the gun into his palm, yet Horatio felt a heat wash over his body. Infinite riches carried a price heavy in bone and blood. Elizabeth had brought him thus far, but the final step— the final choice— was his alone to make.

As the picks, chisels, and hammers pounded away at the concrete, Horatio drew closer to the shadows of the pillars. He watched the men slip small sticks of dynamite in crevices carved from the stone face of the vault. One of the men hummed the opening of the Toccata for the fourth time as Horatio drew back the hammer on the revolver.

~

The dynamite's explosion ripped away the vault's concrete face like an enraged, fiery beast. The blast rippled through the earth and stone, shaking many buildings upon the surface, leaving countless souls terrified. Before Horatio detonated the explosives, Elizabeth dragged the three bodies to safety. Horatio pushed his way through the broken rubble to gaze upon his prize as she straightened out the dead men to leave them looking dignified.

Horatio sat stupefied upon a hunk of shattered concrete inside the vault. A rack of custom-tailored suits, relics of Capone's legendary good taste, caught his eye first. Large teakwood humidors, along with casks and bottles of epicurean vintage, were other luxurious spoils of war. The lockboxes, chests, cases, and even a steel safe stood rank-and-file inside. Daring to investigate, Horatio's trembling hands flipped the latches on a hard leather case. The stacks of greenbacks packed like sardines caused his breath to come in eager, ragged pulses. He dreamt of endless green peppered with heaps of gold and silver in bars and coins. His legs wobbled anew, and he bumped backward into Elizabeth. She stood between him and the exit, surveying the packed room.

"Someone, someday, will find the original vault beneath the Lexington, questing for fame and fortune, but they will find nothingness."

A quickening sense of apprehension seized Horatio's throat. The moment of triumph did not blind his sense of danger, his sense of reality. A woman like Elizabeth could bring him to such riches, so he assumed she could easily take it from him. She had urged him to murder those three other fortune seekers. Would one more body bother her conscience, if she had one? After all, her origin and nature were pure enigmas.

"You are concerned I will betray you— that I will kill you. You do not need to worry. We have many years and much work ahead of us," she glanced back at the dead gangsters. "This is merely our starting point."

"What do you mean?"

"We are going to take this wealth and, as you would say, invest it. Time runs short. We have perhaps five or six years yet, and like the rest of the world we must prepare. Already in the hearts of diplomats and thinkers I see the forecasts of fire and steel. With these riches we will buy and build the means to construct the weapons, the ships, the rolling behemoths, and the other mighty tools of war. In the end, when the world collects itself back together and buries the dead, the scales of power will be changed and we must stand among the new titans."

Horatio was a schoolboy during the Great War, but he heard stories and saw photographs that were testimony from Hell itself. This woman prophesized a new maelstrom of war. Her eyes promised not just a return to Hell but a plumbing of yet deeper malebolges of brimstone than the world had ever suffered. She not only anticipated it, but she seemed to throw her arms wide in welcome to the coming storm.

"What are you? I may not be a church man, but my mother was a religious woman. When she wasn't throwing herself behind the temperance movement, she'd have a belt or two of gin and tell me all about demons."

Elizabeth's face became a mask of quicksilver; her emotions cycled between amusement, regret, and other unreadable emotions. She steadied herself and pressed the issue.

"What do you know of demons?"

"Creatures of Hell, sent to torture, torment, and tempt the souls of men. I shoulda never listened to you! You're some siren from ol' Pitch, ain't you?"

"Perhaps your concept of Hell exists, somewhere. I have never seen it, however, so I cannot say. Demons are not created by some malevolent trickster; they are created by mortal humans. Demons are your strongest emotions and thoughts given physical form."

"So what are you, then? A demoness of greed? Of power or pride?"

"I answered your call, Horatio. You summoned me to the lakeside."

Horatio staggered and propped himself upright on the mighty safe. Hot nausea sapped his strength. Enlightenment left him weak and wounded. Elizabeth took pity upon his tremulous state and filled in the silent void.

"Hopelessness. Despair. Every sincere and heartfelt cry of 'woe is me' is a hymn to my ears. So many broken souls dot the landscape that their collective prayers, in their hearts' crumbling resolve, nourished me into being. The way you cast yourself into oblivion was the final sacrifice needed to 'open the door' for me to enter the mortal world."

Horatio's bloodshot eyes spoke his next question to

Elizabeth's mind, which she answered in her erudite way.

"Many demons are semi-mindless spawns of fear and anger: the strongest and most fleeting of emotions. They simply feed upon their parent emotion, surviving or thriving as they invoke those dread feelings in humans. Mortal despair sustains me and fills me with strength, but I find its taste incomparably bitter and foul. I despise what gives me form.

"Yes, with the tools and weapons we build we will be merchants of despair, carving the spirit from untold masses. It is the only way for me to survive. However, there is much I can offer in return to the world, and to you. Once more, this is only our opening curtain."

Elizabeth picked up Horatio from the ground and held him by the shoulders until his strength returned. Despite the shocking revelations offered of things beyond mortal ken, Horatio thought about how gentle and reassuring her touch felt through his purloined overcoat. He decided to shun the continuing protests of suspicion and trust this demon woman's intentions. He wouldn't mind playing tycoon for a while. Once the chaos and war she foretold had passed, perhaps he could even use his accumulated power to save others from hope's absence... eventually. Besides working towards Elizabeth's grand plan, he had his own comfort to attend to first and foremost. Horatio also found the taste of hopelessness to be bitter, and he resolved to never want for anything again, whatever the cost.

"I think a new life deserves a new name. Something classy, something with kingly prestige," he said. He glanced down at the coat's label, at the monogram for the long-forgotten H.N. "Howsabout... Nightcroft? Horatio Nightcroft."

Elizabeth smiled her assent.

THE BEST LAID PLANS

By

Lydia Ondrusek & John Jasper Owens

Conner Wright's special number— the one he gave women not his wife— sounded its Super Freak ringtone. He swung his office chair to look out on the city skyline and checked the screen.

No way.

Rosemary Taylor. That little gal ran through life throwing commotion and leaving a mess. She could be sweet, though. Sweet as honey— left you licking your fingers even when she was gone.

Conner composed himself, dropped his voice an octave, and picked up.

"Hello, Rose. Long time no squeeze."

An old woman's voice trumpet-blasted his ear. He stood, a reflex from the shock.

"Conner Wright you listen to me. You will arrive at Six Atkinson Circle this afternoon, up north in the county."

"Yes, ma'am," he said, startled into it. "May I ask—"

"Rosemary is having man-problems. Name of Zack Cabrini."

How could someone not screaming be so loud?

"That's what you do, isn't it?" She made it sound as though he shoveled manure for a living.

"Yes ma'am. We're the most exclusive home security firm in the region. If I could just speak to—"

"You wish. Don't come late. I've got my shows before the news."

"Yes ma'am," he said, sweating a little.

"And don't think it."

"Yes ma'am. Um...what?"

"You know what not to think, you're thinking it now. Twitchy ideas about my granddaughter. Twitch-twitch-twitch. Don't bring any of those schemes with you or there will be a reckoning. This is strictly professional and against my better judgment, at that."

Conner started to reply, but the woman had keyed off. He watched the photo of Rosemary, the one he'd taken in a penthouse suite in Las Vegas, fade to menu.

Rose Taylor, he thought, you do get around. Last Connor heard she was in L.A. and in all kinds of trouble— associating with Harvey Wolfe, the sort of thing that gets you on cable news— and now here she was, back in Georgia. She was probably starved for a little nightlife.

All he needed was to get face-to-face with her. Rosemary was a sucker for a good time and he could not imagine any loud, rude grandmother blocking her way. Home security? He'd baffle the old woman and cruise right past her.

Rosemary Taylor, here I come.

~

He found the cottage north of town, and Rose's VW leaning under a maple in the dirt driveway. He left his air-conditioned car thinking about Rosemary, but that old woman! Bekka Zorba confronted him on the front stoop, a chest-high brick of palsied hostility.

"Around back with you," she said, and slammed the door in his face.

He would've tried to peek in a window, but they were shuttered.

There was no path around the house. The beaten little home, surely just four rooms, wore an armor of prickly bushes, crawling vines, and ankle-catching chuck holes. His expensive shoes were getting filthy. Was that a fire ant mound? Sweat ran down his forehead and under his arms. A wasp whined by his ear.

He pushed between two saplings and stumbled forward through sawgrass. Forget this, he thought. Bang on the front door, grab Rosemary, and—

He closed his eyes, dizzy for a moment. Must be the heat.

When he opened them he stood with Bekka Zorba in an untended country jungle behind her cottage. He saw a wide porch and rocking chairs with faded floral cushions. They were on a path, although chinaberry bushes and grape vines hemmed them in, close and thick.

"You think you're so smart," said Mrs. Zorba.

Conner shook his head. How did I get here? "I— no, of course not."

"You think my brainless snippet of an ungrateful granddaughter isn't worth protecting?"

He thought about Rosemary and his stomach rumbled with hunger.

A mouse ran over his Italian loafer.

Bekka Zorba stared at him. The woman leaned over and spat on the ground.

His stomach rumbled again, louder. Conner realized he wasn't just hungry, he was near-starving. When he thought about Rosemary the stab in his gut was a relentless cramp, as though his intestines were twisting. He straightened his tie with damp fingers. Another mouse scurried past his ankle— must be a nest somewhere in the deep weeds.

Conner's head buzzed with a two-scotch-lunch confusion. He gave her the 150-watt smile and began his sales patter. "Ms. Zorba, your home has limited security needs due to its compact size. The most cost-effective thing for you is to hire one of our professionals to observe your property— a two-week contract should do it— until this Zack Cabrini either shows up, or loses interest."

"He won't lose interest," she said.

"Most stalkers do."

The woman turned slowly, careful of her joints, and pointed a claw toward the wooden back fence, a falling-down antique. "You see that?"

"What? You mean the blackbirds?"

The birds rose in unison and flapped away.

"Three blackbirds circling over tomato vines," she said. "They're coming for her."

"Ah."

They stood silently in the still, hot jungle of her backyard.

That cottage, he thought. For no good reason (it didn't resemble the illustrations from his childhood) it reminded him of the witch's house in 'Hansel and Gretel.' He imagined walking up, popping off one of those off-kilter shutters, and biting it. And it... it would taste like... like...

I'm definitely hitting a drive-thru on the way back to the office.

"I bet you expect to be paid well for driving your fancy car out here and talking to me like I'm simple," said Bekka.

Conner put out his hands in protest— all he really wanted, insanely, was a big bite of shutter— but she grabbed his wrist with one hand and, with the other, dropped three coins in his palm.

His hand sagged, and he looked down to see big, rough-stamped disks of solid gold. They weighed about a pound.

He looked up to see her hobbling away.

"A reckoning," the old woman said over her shoulder.

He turned the coins over in the dappled sunlight. Fascinating. There was a cat's head stamped on one side, a noblewoman's face on the other. He brought one coin to the side of his mouth, like a grizzled prospector, and bit it.

No, not gold.

Cheese.

Cheddar, smooth asadero, piquant cantal.

Three yellow wheels of deliciousness.

Still staring blankly at that askew shutter, he stuffed an entire coin in his mouth and chomped like an animal.

~

Zack Cabrini's grandfather had known Bekka Zorba when she was young. Well, known about her. Watched her. Drooled, in all likelihood. The Cabrinis were droolers.

"Oh, she could shake it that one, brown and exotic with all that black hair, like nothing we see around here. Like a gypsy, but rich, rich they were, her family, and she was allus looking down her nose at us townies. And what a nose! It was almost as good looking as the rest of her." Zack's grandfather would make an exaggerated female shape with his hands and laugh until his chortle became an emphysemic wheeze. Then it was back on with the oxygen mask.

He remembered it, after his grandfather died, the stuff about the Zorbas being rich. How could he not, with the bills? He didn't mean to skip on them, but there were so many. He nibbled at their edges, just enough to keep the law happy. When you'd been inside a couple of times it got very important, keeping the law happy. Hard to keep a job, though. With his record, any time something went missing everyone looked at him. Made it hard to steal an honest living.

When Zack met Rosemary he didn't know her granny was Bekka Zorba. All he knew was she liked to wear skimpy halter tops and party down at the Tilt-a-Few. He didn't think about hidden money, he thought about what she was hiding in those Levi's cut-offs. And for a while there, Zack and Rosemary got on just fine.

But that girl was willful. Like a cat, the way they always do what they want and nevermind the man of the house. Or trailer, in Zack's case. And she had money for the Tilt-a-Few, and groceries, but just try and ask her for a little bit for some pot.

She didn't even have a job, where was she getting cash from?

And not even sharing.

So he showed her the back of his hand once or twice. Most all the girls down at the Tilt-a-Few could take a punch. He'd even known a couple to hit back.

But she ran off and got the law on him, that paper that said stay away from Rosemary and her granny's shack. So here he sat, all out of woman and short on liquor. Getting low on funds, thinking about what his grandfather said about Bekka Zorba, the old hermit woman. Everybody knew about hermits and money.

That must be where Rosemary was getting hers.

Zack wiped the side of his mouth.

~

Bekka shook her head, disgusted, as Rosemary searched the pantry for something she wouldn't have to cook. The sight generated a "pfffft!" from the old woman, who began slapping packages and bottles onto the kitchen table.

"What are you doing, Nona?"

"Making what you need."

Rosemary plumped into a chair. Zack Cabrini's grand-father, if he was peeping from the afterlife, had to be drooling. Rosemary Taylor was the image of her Nona as a girl, a Rosalind Russell paper doll lacking only a Hula Girl costume or a gypsy scarf and bangles with little paper tabs. Rose, however, lived a pleasant and useless life which mostly involved men whose accomplishments were celebrated on the walls of the nation's Post Offices.

One of them, Harvey, had left a California prison after considerable greasing of judicial wheels, only to find that Rosemary had absconded with his "retirement fund" of uncut diamonds.

Always a fan of food she didn't have to make, Rosemary reached for the cheese sandwich her Nona had just finished constructing. Bekka smacked her hand with a wooden spoon. "OW!"

Bekka pointed the spoon at her granddaughter and raised an eyebrow. "If you'd had a wooden spoon taken to you a little more often growing up, young lady, you wouldn't be in the trouble you're in now."

"For crying out loud, I just wanted a cheese sandwich, Nona! You said you were making what I needed..." Rosemary nursed her hand, trying to look pitiful.

"Number one, you need more than a sandwich, girl! Number two, I didn't make that for you." Bekka shoved aside condiments and salad and began stacking a pair of sandwiches, this time cutting from a roast redolent with garlic. She piled two thick homemade bread slices high with beef, dripping slices of ruby tomatoes, and icy cucumber. She smeared grain mustard and horseradish on the bread then cut them with whacks of a cleaver, making Rosemary jump and squeak.

She rolled her eyes in bliss over her first bite, however, and forgot to ask Bekka who the cheese sandwich was for.

~

Harvey Wolfe stitched through traffic, tailgating, changing lanes, horn blasting. He was hardly the first man to get suckered by a pretty young thing— Rose Taylor, that girl sure filled out a bikini! — but he was going to make sure this particular one never did it again. He slammed the Porsche into third and peeled off the interstate. This exit would take him to that town she said she came from, where she'd been using her Visa at some cheapjack dive. His info guy said there was only one relative of hers left there, Bekka Zorba on Atkinson Circle.

For the dozenth time he popped open the glove compartment, just to see it. His Walther p22, already suppressed and loaded. When he imagined it, he licked his lips. Pop the old lady. Find the diamonds, Rosemary probably hiding in the bathroom by then.

Kick in the door.

Hey Rosemary. Time to party!

~

Zack Cabrini did come in through the back.

Doing so was a lot more trouble than he'd have liked, but he was covered and hidden and felt safer. He told himself that it was a good start. The possible consequences if he was caught had kept him unable to eat all day. Now his stomach was louder than his footsteps.

The back door was secured, but just a latch— nothing to it. He slid his switchblade in beside the jamb and flicked it up.

It was dark inside, and quiet. He moved into the main room and paused to figure out his next move.

That's when he saw the cheese sandwich.

He tried to turn his head, to think about something else, but the cheese sandwich kept calling him. Not by name, at least, he thought, feeling confused.

Well, there is hunger, and then there is "haven't eaten all day", and there are cheese sandwiches, and then there are Cheese Sandwiches. High, wide, and handsome, that sandwich shone, a fat trophy in the middle of the table. Homemade bread. He leaned over it and took a sniff. He wiped a little drool away. The thought crept into his — no, he suddenly knew, down to his toes— that it would be the most wonderful sandwich he'd ever eaten.

In addition to a disposition toward drooling, the Cabrinis harbored a known difficulty with impulse control.

Zack sat and snatched up the sandwich.

As he savored it, elbows firmly on the table, he became certain that it this was indeed the most wonderful sandwich ever constructed, he began (slowly but accelerating after each bite) to see it as so enormous he would never be able to finish it all. He set the sandwich down on its plate and backed away a little, then caught himself as he almost fell off the table, his claws catching in the wood and his tail swinging frantically till he could hoist his bottom back up.

"Poor little mousie," a voice crooned. "Did mousie get a surprise?"

The lights came on.

A gigantic face framed by wild silver hair hove slowly into view. Zack-mouse cowered. "My house, mouse. My cheese. Belongs to me. You know what belongs to a mouse?" The face began to swim, to change. Fur. Pointed ears sprouted. A pink nose that sniffed him, and a mouth that smiled, exposing dagger fangs.

"What belongs to a mouse is a cat."

In that frozen moment, the back door splintered and a howl of rage vibrated the little house. "ROSEMARY! Where are you, you..." Another crash. Bekka's face went back to normal in a blink. With a quick arm-sweep she threw Zack-mouse off the table; grabbed Zack's clothes and the sandwich half he'd been eating and tossed them in a dark corner.

An enormous man, broad and tall, burst in and stood panting. His reaction to a tiny old woman sitting at a table was to grab her withered arm and shake it. "Where is she? Where's Rosemary? And where's my diamonds!"

Bekka winced, but smiled up at him. "You must be Harvey. Rosemary's told me so much about you." She lifted the plate with one hand, unsteadily, until the other half of the sandwich was under the mobster's nose. "Wouldn't you like a little something?"

Zack-mouse scampered out the ruined back door.

~

Hop, hop, down the wooden stairs.

Dammit, this is all Rosemary's fault.

Zack ran right, then left, then right again. There was a path going back, he remembered, so he stuck near it, a little off in the weeds for cover. His nose twitched.

After a moment his paws felt something different. He was running over cloth. He looked down and saw a nice shirt dropped here in the tall grass. Up ahead another mouse was popping his head out of a leather loafer.

That mouse held the remains of a chunk of yellow cheese in its paws.

It smelled wonderful...

Then, from the cottage, a thump and a yowl that froze the fur on the back of Zack-mouse's neck. Both mice watched as a third came out the back door; a bigger mouse, flying straight ahead like a muddy comet, clearing the steps in a bound.

The big mouse headed down the path, straight for the other two.

Leaping over the remains of the back screen door came a silver tabby whose fur shone in the moonlight.

The cat paused at the top of the stairs and sat tall, sniffing the air. It was nighttime. Playtime. The very tip of her tail beat a rapid tattoo. She looked down into the overgrown kingdom of her backyard and licked her chops.

Three brown mice.

How they *ran*.

HUNGRY

By

Eric J. Guignard

Greg woke at 5:30 a.m. to the chiming ding of his Zen alarm clock, valued at $139. He turned it off. Greg never snoozed. He flung back the black charmeuse sheets, 12-19 in momme weight and $449 in price. The naked blonde lay on her side, snoring. She was $500 and on sale.

Greg slapped her on the ass. "Time to get up, babe. I've got places to be."

The blonde— Barbie (though Greg couldn't remember if that was really her name)— moaned and lifted her arm over squinting eyes. He whistled while checking email on the Apple 4G iPhone plugged in next to his bedside. Skimming his inbox, Greg saw there were only sixty-eight new messages. It was a quiet morning. One email halfway down caught his eye, and he opened it.

To: Greg
Subject: You rule
Message: Yo G-man - Kawasaki accepted your proposal this morning! You got another one!

"Boo-yah!" Greg shouted. He wished Barbie was awake so he could high-five her, but she had returned to snoring.

He strolled into his massive master bathroom, designed with cream and tan marble floors and mirrored vanities, the frames hand-carved from solid wenge lumber. He checked himself out in the mirror and winked; looking fit and fabulous with hair styled every two weeks at the spa.

He undressed and got into the shower.

The sweltering water cascaded onto him. Greg turned on the Sharp's LCD waterproof television, checking stock prices and CNN news while scrubbing his face. He was a busy man, but Greg liked his long showers. He allowed himself a few extra minutes to relax and strategize for the day. There were three meetings lined up and then a sales call. He had a hot new buyer to hire and a pink slip to give to a stagnant executive. Just as he turned the water off, Greg thought he heard the abrupt end of a muffled scream and a thud.

"Barbie?" Greg called out from the shower.

There was no response. He heard nothing else and condemned her for still sleeping. *Must be a nice life*, he thought. *No deadlines, no budget to forecast. Just lie on your back and spread your legs all day.*

Greg wrapped a towel around his waist and checked himself out in the mirror again. He shaved with the latest Panasonic electric laser razor and laid Crest whitening strips across his front teeth. He earned the Kawasaki account this morning and was going after Grainger next. Business had been miserably slow this past week, but he had momentum now. He had his eyes on a new yacht.

"Turn 'em and burn 'em, baby," he said to his reflection.

Greg walked back into the bedroom, thinking he might have time for a quickie. The blonde wasn't in bed any longer.

"Barbie?" Greg asked, caution filling his voice.

Soft lights were on in the room, ambient lamps activated by a timer. Greg picked up the remote stationed next to his iPhone and clicked on the central ceiling lamp. The room lit up, and Greg saw the closet door was ajar, emitting a long, baleful shadow. He swallowed and stepped to the door. The closet was a substantial walk-in, a room of its own, possessing many suits and secrets. He pushed open the door and switched on the closet's light.

On the center of the floor glaring at him was a writhing creature, reminiscent of a terrestrial octopus born of ancient incantations. It appeared squat and bulbous, an angry purple in color, with six misshapen red eyes. The creature was the size of a bulldog, and it waved six tentacles, each a thick, glistening limb with rubber-like suction cups on the undersides, while the tops were coated with claws that narrowed to speared tips like a talon. One large, gaping mouth was situated in the center of its head, surrounded by five additional minor mouths, each fanged and smeared with blood. An expanse of disheveled blonde hair flowed from those mouths as the beast chewed, glaring at Greg.

"Oh my God," Greg whispered in shock. His heart beat furiously, and his hands tighten involuntarily into fists. He took a step toward the creature.

"You damned stupid beast." Anger rose in his voice as he spoke to the thing, like an unhappy parent scolding a rebellious child. "I just closed the Kawasaki account. That means we're merging. Dozens of people will lose their jobs! I'm going to shut down offices in Toledo. Isn't that good enough for you? I made my nut for two months!"

The creature slurped up the last of the blonde hair as if inhaling loose strands of spaghetti.

Greg continued. "You just couldn't wait, could you? Christ. I mean, I feed you every week. You think I sit on my ass in the rain? I'm the one out there busting my hump. I'm the one out there closing the deals. All you do is feed and feed." He paused, then pointed at it. "I had three meetings lined up this morning. You know how much money I can squeeze out of those bums? Now I have to reschedule. I have to clean up after you. People don't just go missing, you know. Someone's going to look for this broad."

The creature closed each red eye in rapid succession and then reopened each likewise. It raised one taloned tentacle and pointed back at Greg.

"Fuck it," Greg said. "I'm going to the meetings."

~

The sun began its long arch across the sky, infusing the city and its labyrinth of freeways with a warm glow. Greg sped down one of those freeways in his Mercedes-Benz CL-Class Sports car. He wanted to feel angry at the monster, but felt a sated contentment instead; a fullness after enjoying a hearty dinner. Today was going to be great, *peachy-a-keen*.

Greg latched on his iPhone headset and speed dialed his secretary. "Sandy, when you get in, schedule a lunch tomorrow for me with Jack Thompson at One Media. Oh, and call my dry cleaners. I need them to pick up an order."

He visualized the day ahead, his successes. He was going to make money. He thought of Michael Douglas saying, *greed is good*.

A wet, rustling sound drifted from behind. Greg looked into the rearview mirror and saw the six-tentacled octopus-creature sitting on the back seat, nestled on the smooth charcoal-grey leather.

The thing had been by his side for eight years. Eight long years since Greg first found it trailing after him, a tiny alien, no larger than a garden snail. It had resembled the sordid spawn that might be produced if a jellyfish humped one of the ghosts from the *Pac-Man* video game. Greg tried to kill it, but it would not die. Greg tried to lock it away in a box, but he felt uneasiness in its absence, a fear, as if he had neutered himself. So he let it follow him for eight years, that nameless thing, growing larger with each day and always hungry.

Of course Greg knew the creature had been with him long before its physical manifestation, lingering in his psyche, growing strong in Greg's desires and deeds. Greg had felt its presence daily inside his mind when he worked in mortgage sales, his first job out of college. He worked with clients who were disabled, clients who were naïve, clients who could not understand English, and clients who were desperate. He lied to them all. He altered papers, and lied about statistics, and made promises that— if ever came true— were entirely by chance. He collected the nice things that men brag about at the golf club house. He cherished his success, and he wanted more, *oh so much more*. Greg grew rich and the creature— the greed— grew along with his bank account.

If Greg thought even further back to when he was a child, he knew the creature was there. He had collected baseball cards and coveted the cards that belonged to Martin, the boy down the block. He wanted to own the best cards, the Reggie Jackson's and the Kirk Gibson's. One day he stole those cards, and when Martin found out, he threatened to tell Greg's mom. Greg punched him in the eye and pulled his hair and made him promise to never tell anyone or he would do much worse. The creature was inside him then, and it was growing.

~

Greg sat behind his mahogany and chrome desk with a ceramic mug of coffee in hand. He drank and surfed the Internet, checking on his favorite stock quotes and porn stars. The wall behind him was glass, providing a majestic view of the city below. When he first earned this office, Greg looked out over the city and admired the view. He was pleased with himself. Now, he could care less about the view, as it didn't make him money or get him laid.

Greg minimized the porn streaming media window on his computer's monitor as the Vice President of Operations sidled into Greg's vast office. "What's up, Roger?"

"Nice work with the Kawasaki account," Roger said and clapped his hands.

"I'm a closer, baby. Just like Baldwin— *Always Be Closing*."

"We should do lunch tomorrow— sushi. Kantaro's has killer Kohada."

"Can't. I'm going to dish with Jack Thompson at One Media."

"Another time then," Roger said.

"You got it, boss." Greg presented a mock salute. The creature was under his desk, and one purple tentacle slithered out from beneath the bottom partition, inching toward Roger's leg. Greg kicked at its gelatinous side, and the tentacle retracted. Roger left the office.

Roger Miller was a career Vice-President, the kind of man who coasts to a lofty position and then sits on his laurels until the golden parachute of retirement floats down upon him. Greg thought Roger was a nice guy, the kind of guy whose kids you'd let play with your own kids. In the business world however, Greg couldn't abide him. Roger spoke about *leadership* and held mandatory seminars in *ethics*. Greg thought they were just buzz words to drop on new recruits and sales reps who couldn't put up numbers. *I didn't meet my budget this week, but I diversified my transformational model of leadership and emphasized my trait characteristic of integrity.* It was such bullshit.

A tentacle caressed Greg's ankle. It was getting hungry. It was always hungry. Greg had to satiate his creature, to feed his greed, lest it lash out on its own. He tapped his phone intercom button. "Sandy, I'm going down to my meeting with AIG."

"Okay, Greg. Your 11:00 a.m. meeting with Susan Patel at Berkshire was pushed back to tomorrow. She wants to make it a working lunch," Sandy said.

"No, I'm meeting with Jack Thompson tomorrow. Damn it, didn't you listen to my voicemail?"

"I'm sorry, Greg, you're right." Her voice went up an octave, which pleased Greg. Her fear of him was very satisfying. "I'll pencil Susan Patel down for the following day. I'll get her confirmation this afternoon. Also, Derrick called in. He won't be in today because his son's sick with the flu bug."

"Tell him not to worry about it. He's fired so he won't have to come in ever again. He's been behind budget all month."

"Yes, Greg, I'll notify Human Resources right away."

Greg tapped the intercom off. He had a big day ahead, big bucks to make. *Turn 'em and burn 'em, baby.*

~

Over the years Greg grew incredibly rich. His influence grew, and his power grew, and, so too, did the creature grow. Greg was never satisfied with his accomplishments and conquests; he wanted more. The beast fed on his greed, and Greg shared its voracious appetite. Their symbiosis fueled a rampant insatiability, the two of them fattening upon the fleeced calves of the world.

Greg rose to Vice-President of Production. He swore allegiance to Roger Miller, but then he sabotaged the collaboration with DuPont, shoveling the blame onto Roger. Roger was disgraced and the Board of Trustees unanimously agreed to fire him. He was a corporate casualty, relegated to early retirement, before he was fully vested. Roger lost his accounts and became destitute and turned to drinking. He wasn't heard from again for a long time.

In the meantime, Greg made more money and, when Greg made money, the creature was happy. When Greg fired people and liquidated accounts, it was happy. When Greg bought bigger houses, faster cars, shinier suits, it was happy.

When the creature was happy, it grew.

Greg went on to seize McKinley & McKinley in a hostile takeover. He made millions. His company's stock holders worshipped him as a financial deity. McKinley's stock holders lost everything. The beast grew. Greg bought out Maxwell. He laid off all company staff— thousands across the country— and outsourced all positions to India. Greg's dividends rolled in, and he bought a jet. The beast grew. Greg paid off corporate spies in each large financial institution in the country. He made the deals. His advisors traded like savages, slaughtering the unwary with cuts across low-performing assets and celebrating with feasts the reward of the mighty. The beast grew yet more.

Its plump bulldog-sized body swelled in mass, fattening until it was the size of a circus tent. Tentacles, once a manageable three feet long, now each extended the length of a school bus. Long ago Greg had been able to hide it, but now everyone saw the beast, and they feared Greg.

Greg burned like a beacon of success, but he was not infallible. When Greg hit a slow spell or a fickle fund veered the wrong way, the beast became hungry and angry. Once in a while, business slowed due to a holiday, or perhaps Greg took a vacation, or caught a cold. Greed never slowed because of holiday. Greed never took a vacation or fell ill. If Greg did not feed his greed, it fed itself. It might consume a casual bystander. It might consume a janitor or a low-producing sales rep. It might consume a tough competitor or even, perhaps, a police detective looking for a missing blonde hooker.

When the creature fed itself, Greg would realize he had been unengaged and thus felt responsible for not minding it. He had achieved the grandest office on the highest floor of the tallest building in the city. He found himself looking out the window now, on occasion, admiring the view for its beauty. When unattended, greed lashed out in ravenous craving, like a crouching trapdoor spider, to snatch up man or woman into one of its six fanged mouths.

Though his greed consumed countless victims, a twinge of guilty revulsion began to hit Greg with greater effect each time. Greg got a hard-on for winning. He controlled markets and willed men to do his bidding. He did not enjoy people's deaths, but his greed had grown stronger than himself, and he could not stop it.

~

The day arrived when Greg's gains grew no more. His profits plateaued. Greg sat impassive in an early morning meeting.

"There are no companies left that we can take over," said Richie, his advisor. "All of our operations are running at maximum efficiency on the leanest staff possible. If you lay anyone else off, it would lead to a decrease in productivity. You're at a tangential margin."

Greg cursed and thought of Roger Miller. You used the big buzz words when you delivered bad news. Good news was jokes, high-fives, and drinks afterwards. Bad news was *tangential margin.*

"Bullshit," Greg said coldly. "Go buy me another jet or something."

Richie nervously shuffled his feet. "But, Greg, we already have a fleet of over one hundred functioning aircraft. There's barely enough passengers flying to make them profitable as it is. Buying another jet would just lead to a diminishing return of our investment."

Diminishing return. More bad news. Greg was now president of one of the largest international conglomerates, and he was being told that he simply could not grow any more. If he wanted to speak to a world leader, he could tell his staff to make the call. If he wanted a law changed, his army of lobbyists overwhelmed the opposition. If there was anything he wanted, he took it. But now there was nothing left to take.

"Have the analysts start up a new enterprise," Greg said.

"What kind of new enterprise?" asked Richie.

"Christ almighty, I don't know, invent something."

"Our research and development team is already wrapped up in inventing spacecraft engineering enhancements, but we won't see those results for another year. Our credit analysts agree the world is in recession right now. It's just not advisable to start up any new companies in the current business cycle contraction that the economy is suffering through."

Business cycle contraction. Greed was not satisfied. It waited outside of the towering office, limbs wrapped around the building in capacious embrace, listening to the conversation. Without warning it thrust one monstrous tentacle through the window, shattering the glass in a tremendous explosion. It plucked Richie— screaming— from the room and shoved him into its central mouth.

"Damn you!" Greg raged at the beast. "That was my senior information advisor, I needed him!"

The creature devoured its meal, drips of dark blood splashing off beaked lips and landing on the edges of Greg's ivory and gold desk. It glared at Greg, always glaring, always judging, and always *hungry.*

"Can't you ever give me some time? I feed you, don't I? Every day, I feed you and feed you. You're constantly on my back, but look at me, I have everything now. I own this company, I own the world! I'm the closer— I make the deals, not you! You can't take something just because you want it!"

Greg paused, considering the bitter irony of his words.

"How many people have you consumed?" he demanded. "When will it stop?"

It glared at him and said nothing.

"I'm through with you," he hissed. "I'm *retiring.*"

The creature closed each red eye in rapid succession and then reopened them one after another. It raised one taloned-tentacle and pointed at Greg.

"I'm retiring," Greg repeated and pointed his finger back at the beast. "You've taken too much from me. You're a bad investment. Go find someone else to leach from."

~

Greg handed in his papers, and the Board approved his resignation. He turned over control of his empire to a collection of various trusts. Greg slept late in the mornings and no longer set his alarm clock. He admired the view from his mansion window, and his greed diminished. He had billions of dollars safely tucked away in multiple institutions, more money than he would be able to spend in a hundred lifetimes. Greg began to give his money to charities and hospitals. He felt a strange new creature form inside him, one of tranquil satisfaction. He even gave it a name, a word he had cringed from in the past. *Benevolence.*

The beast, Greed, still tried to consume people around Greg, but its victims were not enough sustenance by themselves. Its angry-purple coloring began to fade into a pale blue, like a dead fish rotting under the sunlight. The beast gradually shrank, and thinned, and grew lethargic. It could not keep up with Greg anymore.

Greg found moments of peace in the park, staring up at the towering office buildings he once dominated. He knew in those moments that greed was not around.

Since retiring, he had sold his mansion at discount and left the creature behind in the closet. Greg moved to a sensible suburban home and still caught sight of the thing from time to time as it tried to follow him. But, as he sold his assets and gave away more money, the monster, greed, eventually faded.

Greg maintained friendly relations with many of the businessmen he once lorded over. They sought him for consulting work and, occasionally he agreed, if it was for the right reasons. He attended banquets to support the impoverished and spoke at rallies to raise awareness for a plethora of disabilities. He was named a philanthropist and ceremonies were held in his honor so he could dedicate new buildings and artwork. People cherished Greg and sang his praises. Greg donated more money, and people loved him even more. He began to take great conceit in his name and reputation, growing smug as he thought of his legacy and how wonderfully he would be remembered.

He then felt another new creature form in him, one that reminded him of greed and this creature was *Pride*. Greg thought he would not let pride grow, the way that greed had. It was difficult finding a balance between giving away his empire and remaining humble, but Greg succeeded.

One day at the closing of a profitable fiscal year, his former office planned a celebration. Greg was invited and agreed to attend the festivities. He was older now, and nostalgic, and enjoyed the company of his erstwhile peers.

Greg arrived at his former kingdom. People he didn't know waved at him and shook his hand. Greg smiled and chitchatted with men and women he once spat upon. If they had a wedding band on their finger, he told them to say hello to their spouse on his behalf. If they were elderly, he inquired about their health. If they wore a suit, he asked them how business was fairing. Greg could still play the game.

He walked to the elevator, ready to rise once again to the top floor. Following him in strolled his old secretary, Sandy.

"Greg!" she excitedly called out. "It's nice to see you after all this time."

"Sandy— wow— you're looking very well," Greg said.

She wore a form-fitting striped business suit, a power suit, fashionable and commanding.

"It's really nice to see you, too. It's been years."

"Time flies."

"So how's business fairing?" Greg asked.

"This past year was amazing. I work with Roger Miller now. He's on the fast track to regain his Vice-President chair back. The company hasn't made this much money since the day you left."

"Roger Miller, our old V.P. of Operations?" Greg said. "Well, good for him."

"When Roger was let go, he lost everything. His accounts

were dissolved back when you—" Sandy hesitated, glancing at Greg, then continued. "He was a good man, you know. Very trusting. Always concerned for a balance between fair business practice and peoples' well-being. Anyway, he started over again from the ground up. Opened his own company and became a colossal success. Really made the big bucks. We courted him and brought him back here. He's made some great contributions to the company. But... he's changed so much. Roger reminds me a lot of how you used to be... kind of ruthless."

"That's not me anymore, Sandy. I've made a lot of changes in my life. I value integrity now and relationships."

"That's wonderful, Greg. I always knew you were a special person. You were just so single-minded sometimes. Life has so much more to offer than money."

Greg looked closer at Sandy and noticed the warmth in her eyes. They sparkled with an enthusiasm Greg had never paid attention to before, a passion. "Maybe I can take you out sometime. You know, just to catch up."

Sandy nodded and brushed Greg's hand. "I would really like that."

The elevator doors opened, and the two of them walked out into the corporate culture bedlam of the office floor. Across the room Roger Miller, hands upraised, shouted at a group of cringing staff. Greg had expected the mood in here to be joyous; it was supposed to be a celebration. The somber, sullen faces proved otherwise.

Sandy tensed. She ducked down to the long secretary's desk— her old station. "What's happening?" she asked the girl sitting there.

"Oh, Sandy, the Hibachi merger just fell apart."

"What? But it was a closed deal."

"I know. Roger's in a fury. I heard Hibachi found a loophole and is cancelling the whole thing. Roger says he wants to talk to you."

Sandy turned visibly pale and turned to Greg who responded by turning pale himself.

Roger marched toward them and, behind him, slithered a familiar foul, bulbous shaped creature with six distinctive eyes, six mouths, and six clawed limbs.

"I've got to go," Greg muttered hastily and turned back toward the elevator.

"Damn it, Sandy, where have you been?" Roger shouted across the room. "Hibachi screwed us! He screwed us right up the ass!"

But as Roger spoke, his attention was distracted by Greg's hastily departing backside.

"Greg," He shouted. His one-syllable remark commanded Greg to stop, turn, and face him; the man he once ruined.

"Greg," he repeated the name again, rolling the single word around in his mouth in disgust as if he drank a glass of warm piss, expecting it to be fresh lemonade.

"We lost a lot of money today, Greg. Does that please you? Does that remind you of the DuPont deal?"

"I'm sorry, Roger. I really am. I just wish the best for you now." Greg backed up slowly, increasing the distance between them.

"You know what happens when we lose money, Greg. Something gets very, very hungry."

Greg knew what that *something* was. He screamed.

Roger cackled. "Turn 'em and burn 'em, baby!"

The creature crawled toward Greg, raising a thick tentacle and closing and opening each misshapen red eye in rapid succession.

TWISTED WORDS

By

Andrew Stockton

1

I felt uneasy about the whole thing when I drove through the gates toward the distant building. The gently undulating fields on either side of the driveway wore a white early morning mist that swirled and rose, reminiscent of many hackneyed post-war horror films. Images of Vincent Price or Peter Cushing appearing as a black silhouette in the distance flashed through my mind. Yet it was something more than this that provoked this foreboding. No, not foreboding. That would be too strong. Disquiet.

Of course, I put it down to the fact that I had been driving all night from London. As a book dealer I was used to driving great distances but this was a long journey even for me, and I was glad to finally arrive.

The old house disappeared as I drove down a small incline into a corridor of trees and through a carpeting layer of even thicker mist, which gave an eerie impression of unreal trees growing above a cloud of shimmering white. At the bottom of the incline thick branches intertwined overhead, gnarled hands grasping each other over the roadway, supporting each other as if holding up the insubstantial caricatures of decaying life. I was startled to find I had slowed almost to a crawl as I stared ahead at some sort of grotesque death masque: the thicker branches of some of the trees had intertwined overhead and were reaching down in such a way as to produce the shape of a hanged corpse, arms reaching to the throat as if in some vain attempt at release, head lolling to one side and legs and body jerked together in a hideous danse macabre.

I shook myself and sped through, opening the windows to let in the cold air. Back again in sight of the house I felt more reassured, more awake, and I closed the windows as I came to a halt outside the imposing main doors of Malhomme House.

I had met Marco Caldera only once before this weekend, but he hadn't changed at all in those five years. Not that I knew him that well, but we'd always had a close professional relationship and over the last two years it had developed into a solid bond. Marco was a lover of old books and his knowledge of old manuscripts was probably on a par with the best in the business. Where I had turned second-hand book-dealing from a hobby into a struggling business and learned my trade through harsh experience, Marco had always been a foremost expert in the field. He knew the antiques market, too which explained his wealth. In part, anyway. He'd always said he'd been born with more wealth than he knew what to do with. He'd squandered most of it, he'd readily admit, but still remained fabulously rich.

"Anthony, come in, come in, it really is so nice to see you again!"

We exchanged handshakes, smiles, and a brief hug.

"C'mon, lets crack open an Irish. Dianna will see to your luggage." His valet appeared and picked up the one case and overnight bag I'd bought.

"Nice to meet you Mr. Kerslake," Dianna said. She disappeared with them as swiftly and silently as she'd arrived. I was ushered quickly through the hallway and into a room where the flames from a log fire shook the shadows of huge oak bookcases along the walls.

"Wow" was all I could say. This was the first time I had been to this part of the Highlands, the first time I had been to Malhomme House. I had to apologise for appearing so tongue-tied when we sat down with our drinks: I really hadn't expected Malhomme House to be so big, so impressive (he laughed), and I certainly wasn't expecting servants.

"Dianna's more of a necessity than a luxury, Anthony," he explained, "for a variety of reasons. But come on, let's have a refill."

A refill or two later and I was more than delighted with the results of some business we concluded: two crates stashed full of old books and a few objet d'art which would fetch a nice price back in Oxford, plus an absolutely perfect Johannes Nicolai which I felt sure would do well at auction. The rest of the day was spent in a haze, thanks to the Irish whiskey and the heady atmosphere produced by peering through old documents and manuscripts. Before dinner we took a walk around the grounds and, as we walked through the canopy of trees, I was surprised to find how harmless they now appeared. I asked Marco about the hanged man, the strange formation of the branches we were now approaching.

"It is very impressive, isn't it? Most people mention it when they stay. It has a bit of history too— remind me to show you the manuscript of Henri de Mascaal when we get back."

He knew this last throwaway comment would ignite my interest. I was about to bombard him with a hundred different questions but he held my arm to stop me.

"He was hung at this point. *That*—" he pointed up at the intertwined branches "—is the body of Henri de Mascaal. And this spot here—" he moved me gently to one side "—is where all your wishes may be granted. I don't have a wishing well, I'm afraid, but nearly three hundred years ago Henri de Mascaal laid a spell on this place and anyone who desires may make a wish."

"Three hundred years? This manuscript is three hundred years old? Is it on the market, Marco? I'll buy it!"

"It's not for sale, Anthony. Sorry."

I laughed. "Oh yeah? In that case I'll wish for... I wish for fabulous wealth!"

Marco laughed. "That's it, is it? Just fabulous wealth? Not content with a million or two?"

"I'm not too sure how much wealth constitutes *fabulous* wealth. More than I've got now, I know that for sure."

"Well, I hope it comes true, Anthony, I really do." Marco smiled. "Come on, let's get back."

"Tell me more about this Henri de Mascaal. Just what exactly do you know about him?"

An image of Henri the man was already beginning to form in my mind. Not much of an image, it's true; a tall man, muscled, a body forged by hard manual work and a face lined by experience. A face, I realised with a start, not unlike my companion's. My imagination again.

We had stopped. He stared at me, and it seemed an eternity until he spoke again, but an eternity of lives as if we were falling down through the generations from a dim remembered past to the reality of today and—

"This spot has quite a history. Henri de Mascaal came— no, was brought— here to die, so the story goes." He pointed up at the grotesque shape hanging down from the damp branches. "But with a formation of branches like that, which has stood for several hundred years, you would expect stories like that to develop wouldn't you?" His tone became a little distant then. "Only stories, though. Tales from around the fireside; the sort of stories to frighten children when the fires' black shadows scramble a spastic dance on the walls."

He suddenly looked very tired and as he spoke he covered his eyes with his hands and drew them down over his face as if he were wiping away the memory of past tears. He continued

"As if those very shadows are trying to free themselves from their captivity to break through the unseen barrier to enter the world of *living* people, where the noises of the wind outside become the distant cries of the dying or the agonised wails of lost souls."

His words trailed away to silence for a moment, then began again.

"And yet on the face of it, the story ties in with the manuscript." With his mind now thinking of reality, his voice regained its strength. "And the 'script is undoubtedly genuine."

As we walked back to the house, my feeling of disquiet returned, but this time it was tempered by mounting excitement. A three-hundred-year-old handwritten manuscript. This was my idea of heaven.

We were back at the house before Marco would answer any more questions. "Just read the manuscript and make up your own mind," was all he would say.

~

I sat at the table as Marco carefully lifted the manuscript out of its Perspex container and removed an outer layer of muslin. He wore muslin gloves, and his face took on the look of a surgeon preparing for an operation as he laid the first of the sheets of parchment in front of me. A thin layer of perspiration crept onto his upper lip, and his hands shook slightly as he laid it down. I was conscious that I was breathing faster; I was conscious, too, of an urge to touch this piece of living history, but I gripped my hands together and began peering at the fading scrawl.

I knew that the colour had drained from my face. I looked up at Marco and saw his excitement barely suppressed.

"Go on," he urged.

I read.

March 4

God help me, it has been three days since last I saw my daughter. For this reason I have ceased my Journals and my Practices and have set my time to finding her.

Yet search though I will and thoroughly, I find no clue as to where she may be, and with my inner eye I see her lying dead in many places or tortured by some Daemon I myself have raised and loosed from its chains.

And in my dreams too, I see her walking towards me, alive yet not alive, reaching out to me for help, asking with words I cannot hear, touching with hands I cannot feel, yet upon my waking she is gone and yet... and yet I feel her presence so close.

Alas! She is not here. My despair is great, a burden made heavier by the grave weight of my part in this. My heart speaks of my wrongdoing in chastising her ignorance of the Black Arts and speaks of my punishment for meddling with them. Yet I cling to the hope of the hopeless and hope she yet lives. Pah, I banish and summon forces from beyond this life, yet if my daughter still lives I cannot know.

Would that I had never sent her away from me that day. Would that I could trade my own life for hers.

"He must have been frantic," I said as Marco carefully removed the sheet and replaced it with another. He didn't reply.

March 5

My potions have warded off sleep for four days, and I seek still, though I fear my efforts be fruitless.

March 6

It is not of my choosing but I have returned to the Black Arts. I have prayed to the Good Lord this last week but His ears are deaf to my pleas. So I turn to the Power With Many Faces and there seek help.

March 7

Alas! Alas! She is found but lost to me. As the sun set last evening I found her broken body many miles from here. I have carried her home and will lay her to rest if that be the will of the Dark One. Yet I cling to one hope and one hope alone.

I am now prepared, and have made my peace with God. Into His hands I commend my spirit.

"Wow!" I looked up at Marco, expecting to see the same

glow of excitement about him, but his eyes spoke more of sorrow and pain. I couldn't help myself, and before I had truly realised what I had said, the words were out. "Christ, Marco, are you okay?"

For a split second his face changed and I was reminded of a child about to go into their first confession, about to unburden themselves of a terrible secret— but it passed quickly and he laughed.

"Yeah, I'm fine. Sharing this... this..." his hand waved gently over the leaves of parchment "...sharing all this for the first time, it's so... so...."

I'd never known him lost for words. These feelings of unease that had stalked me like a shadow all the time I had been here returned and sat in my stomach like a lead weight.

"Go on, read on," he said.

I begin to understand a little of the hand that guides my Fate. It was not for nothing I have delved into the Black Arts. I see now that I have been prepared for this point in my life, prepared and educated to perform the ultimate Act of invoking the Most Evil One and seeking his help to restore my child.

Yet the Fear within me grows, for I fear the price I have to pay to return my daughter to this world.

It may be I write no more, for it is my belief that the Dark One will seek my own life as payment. Yet know you well that I am willing and ready for this and happily will abandon life so that my daughter live. I can foresee no greater sacrifice on my part. Should it be less than this, I will the more gladly pay.

The rituals must now begin.

May the strength of our Lord protect me, and forgive me, for what I am about to do.

March 14

I continue my writing, but with the broken will of a man who has lost everything.

My daughter lives again though her eyes are dull and her voice silent. She watches my every move and hears me when I speak, or so it seems. At the sun's rise she rises and sits in her chair. At sunset she leaves her chair and retires to her bed. Yet the horror of it is that when I hold her close, her arms are limp, her body is loose and God protect her eternal soul, no heart beats in her breast!

I read and re-read those last few words a number of times. No heart beats... could that really have been the case? Yet though my cynical twenty-first century mind said, 'impossible fantasy!' and my own experience spoke of the substance of reality, yet this— this touched something deeper, a more primitive more spiritual part of me. I sat here, aware of something happening beyond my control, aware of the cold sweat that now covered my body, of the unexplained fear that made me look around the room.

March 20

I record this now as testament to my betrayal of our Lord and to my foolishness. I record this also so that it may serve as warning to others who may wish to take the Left Hand Path into the Dark World. Would that I had never been born so that my actions would remain undone.

I will continue to record it within this diary, so that the true events will be told as they occurred and please God none other follow my ill-thought designs.

Every day, every long hour that passes, she watches me. I can no longer call her my daughter for she is unknown to me.

She will not eat, but in my heart I know the reason for it. Every day her skin falls closer to the bone, every day her eyes become more sunken. Her fingers are now blackened at their tips, wrinkled and cracked, her toes also. I hold her hand and she watches my hands upon hers; yet I fear to do that now, for I feel the failing strength within and it horrifies me.

Never is there the look of recognition in those lifeless eyes, never the hint of love as there once was. Oh, but I cannot think of things as they used to be, for that brings on the pain and the pain is too great for me to bear. She watches me now with barren unseeing eyes even as I write these words.

This then is the price I have to pay for my foolishness. My daughter condemned to a slow living death and I, the perpetrator of the crime, must watch every long agonising moment of her decay.

March 25

This cannot continue. Surely such monstrosity cannot exist in the face of our Lord?

Her skin decays and is become discoloured. Her lips are drawn back from her yellowed teeth and her neck is torn and cracked, unable to support her skull so that if she moves it rolls upon her shoulders like an ill-made child's doll.

Her hair, scant as in leprosy, grows only in the clumps between the rotting wounds upon her skull and of the rips and tears upon her arms and legs I cannot speak of fully for though I clean them daily still there appear the maggots that gorge themselves upon the flesh or being fat with flesh fall off onto the ground.

She no longer hears my words nor looks my way. Still at dawn she rises and at sunset lays herself down but not to sleep for no sleep touches the place where once her eyes were. And I, in such sleep as I have, dream of her as she once was, so that when I wake I cry to dream again.

No, this cannot continue.

March 26

It is done, though 'twas not an easy duty. I have prepared her resting place, a grave beneath the hanging branches of the trees where as a child she used to play. I believe her soul, such as it may be now, would like that, and it is this thought that gives me both some little pleasure and a great strength with which to perform this task. God forgive me, for I must murder her a second time.

But oh, from what heart does murder spring? From what heart does love? Can they truly be the same? Do both hearts beat together within me, in delicate yet deathly time?

As she lay upon her bed did I take the consecrated waters and the stake. Having marked the pentagram in salt about that place where I stood I blessed the stake and thrust it with all the might God gave me through the rotting carcass' breast.

Such was the hideous scream that vomited forth from her gaping maw that I lost hold of the stake and fell forward upon her. Her ribs crack'd like thin icicles beneath me, my hands pushed through the festering liquids held within her breast so that they spurted along my arms, burning the skin with the pain of the fires of Hell itself. Her hands, by accident or intent I know not which, came about my throat and held there with a grip I had not felt since she lived.

I could not breathe nor utter any cry for the strangling bones held tight about my throat and the curling yellow nails ripped deep into my flesh. The fingers dug into my neck so that my muscles tore, and with such force that the decaying flesh upon their ends was forced off and only bone gouged deep into my flesh.

As my vision darkened and I felt the welcoming onset of unconsciousness, I feared this would be my end, but its strength then surely waned for I woke some time later upon the floor beside the bed.

I had little time, for much of the day had passed, and her burial must be performed before darkness.

I carried her to her grave and did cry for her, or for this thing I held, I know not which; the carcass was broken, limp and so very light in my arms. The jaw clacked against the skull as I carried it and the legs swung jerkily with my movement.

I laid her down beside her grave, beside the pure white robe and the Holy Bible I had left there in readiness.

This then was my daughter, or was the House where dwelt her Soul while yet she lived. I held her hands together in mine, now accustomed to the movement of the tiny worms beneath her skin and the putrid flesh that fell at the slightest touch.

I laid her robe upon her and laid her down into her final bed. The ceremony complete, the earth filled, I laid me down upon her grave and wept until I slept.

April 2

I thought the deed complete but it is not. Each night it attempts return, each night the nearer it gets.

The first night did she rise from her grave and stand in eerie silhouette against the cold moon, hands reaching out to me. Yet I know no moon will rise for some nights and there was no moon that night, so dream it must be. The next night did she walk towards this very house. So plain were these visions that on the morrow I returned to her resting place, a great fear in my heart that I would find the ground there disturbed. Thank God, 'twas but a dream!

The third night she came to my window and did slap her hands against it to waken me. I awoke and opened the shutters to her. She reached in to take my hands and there was life in them and warmth and love in her eyes. And I cried for she lived. And I held her to my breast. And hugged her. And felt the bones crack and when I looked again it was her blackened sunken corpse I held.

Then it was I awoke.

Then on the fourth night it came again but I would not let it in and fear of her held me so I could not move.

And she turned her back to me and spread her arms and cried loud and long into the death-black night, her evil wail rising to a sky streaked with luminous cloud. And from the trees distant came answering calls. Then came for me others of her kind; the long dead, the newly dead, the hideous and the pretty, ever nearer.

And I could not wake, nor move, but lay fearful as they gathered at every window and door. Their screaming drowned the beating down of the doors and covered the sound of the splintering of wood at the windows, and in they came. Crawling like vile snakes upon their bellies I could see no movement but plainly I heard them as they came closer, could feel them reaching out for me. About my bed they came, scraping and touching. And still I could not move. Their wailing waxed and died and came again, the pitiful yet hideous screaming from jaws that were both open and closed until she who I once nurtured did drag the sheets that covered me off my bed and onto the floor. And they squirmed toward me and their wailing slowly died. Then it was silent and they began to climb onto my bed. Their weight upon me was crushing so I could not breathe and still they came, all struggling to climb one upon the other. They spoke then, clearly but within my mind they spoke and I heard each of their voices fill my head, the young, the aged, the shrill and the hoarse, all spoke as one

'You are one of us now. We have come for you, immortal.'

Their bodies crushed hard against mine, the fetid smell of decay filled my being. One head crushed close to mine, so that its unseeing socket pressed hard against mine own eye and dripped its vile containment onto my face. Their weight stopped my breathing, and I floated into the darkness. I was being carried out into the night where the air was ice on my face. Carried to my daughter's grave. I struggled for I feared these unholy ghouls would bury me with her, but as if bidden by some unearthly power they lifted me to the trees and strung vines about my neck.

I hung there until my lungs burst within my chest and the blood burst out of my head, and the thing that was my daughter stood beneath me, until darkness took me, easing the pain but not the fear.

I was dead. But for my deeds I had not entry to Heaven, where my daughter watched in sorrow. My corpse was torn down by the grasping hands of these undead, and they cast me down. Down I fell into the grave where my daughter lay, and she did put her arms about me and others of her kind did throw down earth upon me and fill the grave. Such were these dreams or visions.

I have taken this as Prophecy. I pledge that before this day's end I will commit myself into the hands of Our Lord.

I write my last here and will leave this life trusting in the charity of My Creator that He will not condemn my soul for my deeds. Thus it is I will take my life when my words here are finished. Thus it is I will go the place where my daughter lies, and from the trees above will end my earthly existence. My suicide will be my final payment. I have the rope before me, and I feel in my heart this to be the right path to follow for, though I fear death and fear for my immortal soul, I fear this coming night the more.

My affairs now are in order, and I will place my papers with the Holy Bible so that they may be kept safe until they are found. My hands shake now, so that my writing is hard to read yet I am determined and must complete this record.

The ground wherein my daughter now does lie I have graced with a charm: let each man who stands there have but one wish, and that wish be granted whether it be for good or evil yet.

~

And there the manuscript ended.

I knew there was no way Henri de Mascaal could convey the full intensity of his emotion at that time, nor was there any way in which I could hope to understand what he was going through. To a certain extent this was all so remote, a manuscript written hundreds of years ago by someone I had never met: a fascinating historic document, certainly, but nothing more than that.

Then why were my eyes filled with tears? Why was my stomach knotted so tight and my fists clenched so hard on the table I could hardly move? The room felt hot, overly oppressive, and I was sure I sensed the smell of decay. The words on the manuscript moved in and out of focus, the shapes of the letters seemed to squirm in front of my eyes as I began to feel light-headed. I knew I should get up and get out of that room, with its enveloping sense of death, but my legs would not respond and I could not move. The weight on my shoulders spread up into my head. The roar of pounding blood filled my ears. Sweat dripped down my face onto my chin and I was faintly aware of the taste of salt in my mouth.

I tried to squeeze my eyes shut, but the swirling words were still there, shapeless and meaningless. The growing stench of rotten flesh filled my nostrils. Nausea swept up from the pit of my stomach, and though I tried to breathe slowly, though I tried to regain some composure, all I was aware of was my whole body enveloped in sweat, a shroud for the nausea that filled me as completely as the stench of rotting flesh filled the room. Blackness shimmered around the edges of my vision. My whole body vibrated as if I was about to pass out. All I was conscious of was the smell and taste of putrefaction as if the whole room had become a coffin, *my* coffin, and there was only that and the blackness.

And the footsteps.

Through the sickness, the decay, the sweat, the pounding in my ears, through all of this I was aware of light footsteps behind me. I knew that turning around would be useless, but I was afraid of that rhythmic hushed slap of bare flesh on the floor. I was faintly aware of the taste of blood in my mouth, and the slow dribble of it down my chin. Fear filled my being. Fear, stench and the footsteps.

I knew it was *her*. I knew that she walked through the thickening air of the room toward me. All the descriptions of decay weaved in front of me as I began to slip, sliding on the thin ice of my own sanity, losing my footing on the cliff edge, falling off the highest ledge, slipping, tripping, from dream to nightmare, plummeting and through it all the footsteps came closer and closer.

Her bloodless hands reached out, their scant flesh black and loose, stretched out to touch me.

A brief, flickering image of some insubstantial, decomposing corpse reaching out toward me slashed across my mind, but it was the hands placed firmly on my shoulders that made me cry out. The pressure of the grip on my shoulders increased, and I was aware of being lifted. The light in my eyes was blinding, but the smell of smoke, *log-fire* smoke, dispelling the stench of decay, was something wonderful and pure, almost holy, and I breathed it in deeply and quickly. The salt liquid in my mouth caught in the back of my throat, and I coughed. As my eyes focused I saw Marcos' face staring down in concern.

"Let's get you outside," he said, though the words meant nothing to me. They were as unreal as everything else my vision took in.

He lifted me back onto my feet and my shaking legs barely took my weight. The world around me swayed, but at least it was the real world, the world I knew.

"Fresh air will do you good."

A few tentative steps in the cool breeze and my strength came flooding back: to be honest I was surprised how soon I felt normal— and rather foolish— again. We walked outside for a while, each in our own silent thoughts. Marco's face more often than not watching me with concern.

"I'm sorry, Marco, I—"

"Forget it. The room was decidedly hot and with everything... guess you were pretty close to fainting."

I couldn't muster much more than I weak, "Yeah."

Marco seemed content to let it pass. I couldn't really tell him what I'd experienced: how in the name of God could I tell him that *she* was in the room with me? He'd probably put it down to imagination. I probably would too, in a couple of weeks, or months.

~

That evening was the last before I had to travel back to London. We discussed aspects of the manuscript, at some length, I read through it several times, each time with no obvious ill effect. I offered to buy it several times, but was refused with a consolation promise of first refusal on it if ever he decided he'd sell.

Too much Irish again that night saw me sleep past breakfast the next day. Having missed breakfast, Dianna packed me a huge hamper for the drive. Marco was very concerned that I had recovered from my fainting experience and was fit to drive, but I assured him quite easily on that score.

I thanked them both for a wonderful visit and Marco for his special generosity. We made promises not to leave it so long again and I climbed into the car.

"Have a safe journey back, Anthony," Marco said. He shook my hand for the last time as Dianna put the hamper in the back and closed the boot. Then he smiled, "Oh, and remember your wish. Let us *all* hope it comes true!"

I laughed. "Yeah, let's hope so. Okay, take care Marco, and see you soon."

That end of a holiday feeling came over me as I drove away. I had to admit I was quite sad to leave. But the place still had one more surprise for me.

I drove slowly at first, window down, cool air, fresh and pleasant, blowing through the car. I'd been waving out of the window and watching them grow smaller in the mirror. One last wave, I closed the windows and was about to give it a bit more throttle. I looked in the mirror to see them both one last time, and saw them, small and distant yet surprisingly clear watching me and waving as I drove away.

But it wasn't them. I knew who they were, of course, or felt sure I did. The man seemed older, much older, more frail; the woman younger, but broken, twisted, almost, almost—

The car bumped off the drive onto the grass. I focused

again and saw only Marco and Dianna turning back into the house. I manoeuvred back onto the road and settled back for the long drive home, the hair on my neck risen, my palms sweating and a feeling of disquiet and unease upon me that took a good few hundred miles to fade.

2

The ground wherein my daughter now does lie I have graced with a charm: let each man who stands there have but one wish, and that wish be granted whether it be for good or evil yet

I had good reason to remember those words. In the two years since my visit, I became a very wealthy man. I was a little puzzled by this, because I didn't normally believe in good luck charms, or wishes coming true, but in this case I was forced to make an exception.

Business had flourished. So much so that I'd opened another shop in Oxford, one in London and two more on the South Coast. I seemed to have developed a knack for being in the right place at the right time: every so often a rare or valuable work dropped into my hands. For example the last few days saw a first edition Edward Coke and a copy of Vocabularus Utriusque Juris pass through, leaving behind a healthy profit. I had several wins on the Lottery— not overly massive, but under normal circumstances they'd be considered lifestyle changing wins— and even staked a little here and there on the horses or at the Casino. I must admit I thought this would be chancing my luck too much, but my fingers did not get burned, and each time I came away with more than I expected. I even— and this is the hardest fact to accept— discovered that relatives hitherto unknown to me had died and left small fortunes.

I've gone into property now, too. That's definitely a lucrative area. Yeah, it's definitely been a very lucky two years.

I kept in touch with Marco of course, though I haven't seen him personally. I have been far too busy with one thing and another and he's been out of the country for most of the last year. I thought of arranging to meet again soon, but - well, there never seemed to be enough time. Life's busy, but not too busy and I was enjoying the benefits of wealth. I sometimes sat and wondered just how much wealth *'fabulous wealth'* was. Not very often, though. I was too busy making it and spending it to worry too much about that.

~

I wasn't usually at home to receive the post.

My secretary generally read it and emailed anything to me wherever I was: my apartments or offices in Rome or Manhattan or any of my stores across Europe or the States. For some time, however, I'd felt in need of a break. My empire had grown phenomenally over the past five years and I'd spearheaded the whole show myself. *Kerslakes* was one of the finest, most respected names in the collectables market and dealt in old books, memorabilia, antiques, anything that was over a specific value and which could be bought or sold. *Kollectibles* was a chain of more down-market stores that traded in anything antique regardless of price. Kerslakes and Kollectibles had very separate identities: that way we had most areas of the market covered, and business was booming.

And so, today, and for the last few weeks I had been at home and to be quite honest, I was enjoying the break from routine. I kept in touch with the business of course, but this was a well-earned break. For the last two years or so I'd been making wealth but not really spending it:

which after all is what it's all about. I was recharging my batteries, and damn well enjoying it.

When the post came this morning, it was the usual pile. Business correspondence I could pass on to my secretary, junk mail that went straight in the shredder along with offers of business partnership and potential investments for my fortunes. But there was one small parcel that stood out.

The handwriting was vaguely familiar; the postmark was illegible.

There was a small letter and a parcel. From Marco. Christ, I hadn't seen him in years and to be honest I felt a bit guilty. I was always thinking I should arrange to visit again, or invite him to London, but there never seemed the time.

I read through his letter and my excitement grew by the word! He hoped I was well and had enjoyed watching my career flourish. He wished me continuing success. Planning on leaving soon, he would be away for some time and because of this there was a document of special interest he wanted me to have.

My heart thumped in my chest and images of that weekend in Scotland came flooding back. It couldn't be true, could it? He was giving me the manuscript of Henri de Mascaal?

My hands shook as my fingers tore at the accompanying parcel. I tried not to rush, not to tear wildly at the brown paper. As soon as I saw the bubble wrap inside, I ripped the outer envelope off then took a deep breath and carefully opened the wrap. Despite my excitement, I deliberately refrained from opening the grey plastic document holder.

Instead, I prepared as I would for any other rare artifact. Gloves, covering sheets, the self-sealing container, small brush....

Taking the document out brought back all the memories, and something of the experience I had felt when I first read it. Images swept through my mind....

"I saw her walking towards me, alive yet not alive.... I felt her presence so close.... I prepared her resting place, a grave beneath the hanging branches of the copse...."

I read on to the end and breathed a silent prayer of gratitude to the man who laid his charm at the site of his own suicide. Even though I no longer believed in the power of that wish I made— time proved to me that it was more than just luck that had given me my wish for fabulous wealth— I felt it appropriate I should acknowledge him in some way.

It was then I noticed one further sheet of manuscript under a small sheet of paper holding some words in Marcos own handwriting.

Anthony, this last page may have been missing. I enclose it now to complete the words of Henri de Mascaal. Think of me in your time to come. Marco.

In your time to come. Strange phrase to use. I re-read the last paragraph of the previous page and began reading the new page

The ground wherein my daughter now does lie I have graced with a charm: let each man who stands there have but one wish, and that wish be granted whether it be for good or evil yet.

Yes, I knew this, but as I read on my blood ran cold and a chill sweat covered me.

The ground wherein my daughter now does lie I have graced with a charm: let each

man who stands there have but one wish, and that wish be granted whether it be for good or evil yet.

Let each man know that his wish bears a price that must be paid.

So was it that the price paid for my wish for my daughter's life beyond death was my own eternal, enduring grief, so let it be with this. Let he who would make a wish do so with wisdom; let the fool wish with ignorance, for the price of any wish is the immortality of his God given soul.

Immortality!

Terror overtook me then, but I could not really understand why. It was as if my unconscious mind grasped the full horror of Henri de Mascaal's words, but my conscious mind could only grasp at fragments of the truth. And then, as if with a jigsaw, the pieces began to come together.

Immortality had its price. This was Henri de Mascaal's immortality; a life lived forever with only the undead as companions. My heart raced and a violent urge to vomit overtook me so that I turned sideways and spewed violently across the carpet. I heard myself moaning, long and pitifully, as if it was coming from someone else, someone far away. For a long moment I thought I was near nervous collapse as the edges of my vision darkened, my arms and legs tingled and I tried in vain to focus hard on the words before me.

And then I heard them.

Hardly audible, a noise something like distant traffic, but growing louder, becoming slowly more distinct: I had been kneeling on the floor, rocking to and fro but now my moaning stopped as I strained to listen. I realised with a shock that hit me as hard as any kick in the stomach that the sounds did not come from outside. Though they were most definitely outside the apartment, and I could hear them approaching, the sounds were inside my head. Closer and closer they came. I heard them all, scrabbling at the door of my apartment, scrabbling at the splintering wood, standing behind me, so frightening, so horrible, so... so damned.

And as the words took shape within my head I began to scream.

"You are one of us now, we have come for you, immortal."

In a chair in the Library of Malhomme House, Henri de Mascaal gave a silent prayer of thanks to God and at the end of his long existence closed his eyes for the last time.

STORBECK'S GOLD

By

Cory J. Herndon

Jimmy Storbeck knew two things at the moment of his death. The first, easy to dismiss now, was that he was not a very good bank robber. The second was that his sweet, sad saint of a wife, the woman who'd stuck with him through six potentially life-ruining months in the penitentiary, would be taken care of. His partner Mitch had the bag, the bag filled with tightly wrapped tens and twenties. Half of that would find its way to Jimmy's wife in her time of desperation, and she would never have to want or worry about anything again.

There were many things Jimmy didn't know. He didn't know Mrs. Storbeck as completely as he thought. He didn't know how well sound carried from his basement den into the upstairs bathroom. He didn't know about the reward she'd arranged with the police for turning him in, leading to the ambush at this gas station less than a minute after he'd called her from a payphone to tell her he was alive. He couldn't know how badly she wanted to use that money to get away from people like Jimmy Storbeck.

Not that she'd ever see the reward. She twisted open a wine cooler to pass the time while she waited for the detectives. Her eye on the bottle, she took a step toward the living room and slipped on a cat toy that rolled underfoot. As she fell, the back of her head struck the blunted snout of a cast-iron toad—a grinning amphibian gargoyle doorstop

Jimmy had never liked all that much—and severed her spinal column on the thing's upturned nose.

Technically, Jimmy Storbeck would die a widower. He definitely didn't know that.

Mitch Lewis, his partner, was in the getaway car, his mother's 1988 Thunderbird. As he fled the bullet-riddled gas station he saw Jimmy in the rearview mirror raising his hand in farewell. Then the pumps erupted into an inferno that engulfed Jimmy Storbeck, several police officers, an attendant, a man who had stopped off for a pack of gum, and several other buildings on the same block.

Mitch should have been happy about this explosive event. (Though the cops had caught up to them at the gas station, he had emerged unscathed and gotten away with the loot.) But he wasn't. He really had liked Jimmy. They were friends, worked together on smaller jobs, and had been planning this last one for months: the big score, an idea they both knew was bullshit but neither could resist. Now Jimmy was gone and Mitch grieved. Worse, he could be in big fucking trouble. A robbery was one thing, but he'd just left a lot of burning corpses in his wake. If the law caught up to him now, someone would have to pay for all those dead people, and that someone would be Mitch Lewis.

In the side mirror he saw a spray of liquid splash from the rear of the T-bird. Who knew how many shots that missed him had struck the Ford's gas tank. Unlike in the movies, the car didn't explode. It just ran dry and the trail of gas would follow him. The sirens he could already hear barreling toward the gas station would soon be heading his way.

Staying in the car was suicide, even if it wasn't already sputtering. Carrying the duffel wasn't much better, but if he could cut through some backyards and reach a road heading out of town toward Ocean Beach Highway, he could get to the woods on the edge of town. Mitch felt certain he could find a trail there, and spending a few nights in the woods wouldn't be a problem. He'd been through far more rugged situations growing up in this place.

Best not to leave the car intact, he thought. His eyes fell upon the trunk of the Thunderbird, where his grandmother still carried a pack of industrial-strength road flares. They burned insanely hot, and nothing could blow them out. When they were kids, Mitch and Jimmy used to build campfires with them. He grabbed two—just for insurance—and ran as far as he thought he could throw. Already he could see the fire trucks arriving at the gas station inferno; he saw police cars, a flashing, blinking mob that was moments away.

Mitch popped the cap of the flare and struck the end against its rough surface. As it sputtered to life with blinding pink light, he hurled it at his former getaway car. The gas ignited and raced toward the bleeding vehicle's tank. Mitch was already hauling ass down an alley. He thought for a moment a barking dog would bring an end to his escape. Then the Thunderbird's tank exploded and every dog for miles joined in the cacophony.

By the time he reached the road leading to the highway, Mitch almost smiled. The sirens weren't getting closer. He hauled the duffel back onto his shoulder and set off down the road, invigorated by terror and the dawning realization that he'd made it. The money was his. *Those are the breaks, Jimmy.*

David Parsons was not looking for Mitch in particular. He was not all that fussy about whom he stopped to pick up alongside the road. He was just looking for some company. Anybody would do. David would talk to them, learn from them, feed them, but never touch them, never frighten them. Then, when they'd fallen asleep, he liked to cut out their hearts.

Ahead on the shoulder of the two-lane road David spied a man coming the opposite way on the right shoulder, a lanky man in dark clothes carrying a duffel bag that looked like it outweighed him. David saw the explosion up the road a ways past the man. Beyond that another huge conflagration near the center of town. What unexpected happenings.

David pulled up alongside the man, who eyed him with cautious gratitude through the passenger window. The man's face was spattered with blood, but either the man didn't realize or didn't care. David stretched across to unlock the door. As the bloody man maneuvered the bag onto his shoulder and pulled himself up, David saw the silver flash of a semiautomatic pistol tucked into the back of his pants. The elastic waist of the man's hooded sweatshirt had gotten snagged on the gun-sight. He doubted the man could have drawn the weapon cleanly and fired.

David offered his hand after the door closed. "Hello," he said. "My name is David."

"Are you heading out of town?" the man said by way of introduction, shaking David's hand without making eye contact.

David nodded.

"Name's Mitch," the man said. "I, ah, don't know what happened with all the—with the fires."

David was certain he was lying, but didn't really care. He shrugged to let Mitch know so.

"David," Mitch continued, "any chance you're heading back the way you came? I just need a lift out Ocean Park Highway. I have a friend there... I'm staying with."

Though David only listened to this explanation so he could plausibly reference it later, he grinned and said, "How'd you know I live out that way? I'd just been planning to hit Safeway for a quart of milk, but all things considered, might as well head back. Who needs milk when you've got a fridge full of beer?"

"Right," Mitch said, but didn't pick up on the implied invitation. David's lower lip twitched momentarily, then his smile returned, thinner than before but still sincere. He'd practiced.

"So, staying out Ocean Beach?" David asked as he

whipped the truck around at a wide intersection. "Anyone I know? Maybe I could give 'em a call for you?" He waved his cell phone.

"Probably not," Mitch said too quickly. "They haven't lived there long. Just renting, probably moving out soon." With painful nonchalance he shifted one leg to cover the gap where the bag's zipper seam had torn, the simple act revealing the bag was stuffed with bloodstained stacks of cash.

David drew an involuntary gasp. His personality tended toward expensive entertainment. For the first time since he had begun hunting the people of this small town, taking one or two every year, he found himself in a rush to kill.

David turned off the wide avenue heading toward Ocean Beach and turned down Twelfth toward the decaying suburbs. There a meth epidemic kept police too busy to worry about a new, freshly waxed Chevrolet pulling to the curb in front of a nondescript house with plywood over the windows. A house that had stood empty since the owner had accepted a ride in the new, freshly waxed Chevrolet. David had decided to keep up the payments and insurance on the house, since the owner had no survivors (he made sure of that personally). He found it useful to have a house in town sometimes, especially in a part of town no one wanted to visit.

"Where are we?" the man asked. "The highway—"

"I need to check in with my aunt," David said smoothly. "She doesn't get many visitors anymore, so I stop by every week. Ten minutes. Would you like to come in?" Seeing Mitch's reluctance, he added with uncanny sincerity, "She bakes. I guarantee you a plate of cookies. Probably apple pie, too."

"Doesn't put the pie out on the windowsill though, huh?" the man asked, nodding at the plywood.

"That just happened last week," David lied. "We're getting them fixed in a few days. Kids."

Mitch stared suspiciously at the windows. "Knocked

them all out?"

David laughed. The sound was forced. His performance was off. The money was *right there* hurry up hurry up.

"Come on, take a load off. We'll get you out Ocean Beach in plenty of time."

"All right," the man said after a few more nervous moments. "Mind if I bring my luggage? Hate to leave it out on the street, even in a truck like this. No offense, but your aunt lives in a pretty shitty neighborhood."

"It wasn't always," David said, unexpectedly defensive. This cretin didn't deserve to even hold that much money.

Mitch said, "After you."

David led the way, approached the porch, and reached into his pocket for the door keys. To Mitch's suspicious look, he said, "She doesn't always hear the bell, and I'm not going to make her walk all the way to the door on her arthritic legs. Jesus, Mitch. What do you think, I'm some kind of serial killer?" He laughed.

"Serial killer," Mitch said. "Right. That would be pretty ridiculous. After you then, Mr. Bundy."

"Bundy only killed women," David said.

Mitch arched an eyebrow, but stepped up beside him, letting the bag slide from his shoulder.

The man was almost inside the house. The *money* was almost inside the house.

The door opened, revealing in the fading light of the setting sun a dark but tidy interior. David reached in to flick the light switch, a piece of dumbshow. The lights didn't work, of course. "Damn it, she must have forgotten to pay the bill." He added a heavy note of concern as he said, "Least, I hope that's all it is. I'm going to check her room." He waved toward the dim shape of an open doorway. "Could you find your way to the kitchen over there? There ought to be candles in one of the drawers near the sink."

"Sure," Mitch said, and David could tell he'd let his instinctive concern for an imaginary little old lady override his suspicions when the man set the heavy duffel bag in the corner next to the door. As Mitch slipped past him in the dim sunset light, David reached to his own waistband and drew a long hunting knife. The blood gutter along the blade would help quickly open the vein of a struggling animal, and it could open a heart-sized hole in a man's chest in less than a minute.

David reached out to tap Mitch's shoulder before he was out of reach. The man spun around in surprise, his eyes flashing gold with the secondhand reflection of the dying sun—but the scream stopped before it could begin. The blade plunged into the soft tissue just below Mitch's solar plexus, knocking the wind out of the bank robber before tearing through organs and arteries to puncture his heart. Mitch spat up blood, spraying David with saliva and gore.

The door clicked shut behind them. David twisted the knife.

As Mitch's life flowed out along David's arm and onto the floor of a dead woman's living room, the man released a last dying sputter. He twitched and flailed at the gun in his waistband, knocking it free from his belt, but the sight snagged on his sweatshirt. One final spasm, and he clutched the weapon's trigger, shooting himself in the buttocks as his last conscious act.

Mitch Lewis died in terrible and embarrassing pain.

~

"Baker 4-2-1, we need you to divert from the gas station fire. Possible 2-46 near your location, multiple reports of firearms discharged in the residential area of the twelve hundred block south between Hemlock and Monticello."

"Copy that, dispatch, this is Baker 4-2-1. We are on our way, over," Officer Larsen replied into the mouthpiece.

After the dispatcher acknowledged, he flicked on the patrol lights and said to his partner, "Well, *this* couldn't be meth-related."

"Surely not," she replied.

"Don't call me Shirley," Larsen said without missing a beat, eliciting an undignified snort from Officer Ringley. He picked up the mouthpiece and replied, "Dispatch, this is Baker 4-2-1 again. We're a few blocks out. No sign of any disturbance, but we'll take a closer look."

"Roger that, Baker 4-2-1. Proceed with caution."

"That's a 10-4, dispatch. Baker 4-2-1 out." Larsen replaced the mouthpiece and shot one of his best 'aw, shucks' grins to his partner.

She was a rookie, but Larsen hadn't complained when Ringley was assigned to him. Something nicer to look at for once than his last partner, a flatulence-plagued behemoth named Scott. Larsen was as happy to see Scott's ass depart to a lifetime mall security work as he was to see Ringley's sweet can shimmy into the passenger seat every day. From the looks she'd sent his way for the last few weeks, Larsen suspected she didn't mind having a new partner either.

Larsen turned onto Twelfth at Hemlock. He took it slow; the four-lane street that hadn't seen repair for nearly a decade and a half—potholes everywhere, some still half-filled with gravel—and God forbid a civilian should jump out at the wrong time. There were no businesses to be seen, but plenty of run-down houses with overgrown lawns or wooden fences covered in flaking white paint. Not the sort of neighborhood people walked through, but drove past as quickly as they could.

A pale, middle-aged woman in a halter-top and shorts stood on the sidewalk waving her arms as they approached. She wore no shoes.

Larsen and Ringley parked several yards from the woman and approached on foot. The woman was twitchy, with telltale scabs that marked her as a meth user. Larsen rested his hand on the pommel of his nightstick as he approached, and noted from the corner of his eye that Ringley did the same.

"What seems to be the trouble, ma'am?" he asked.

"Th-there," the woman stammered, eyeing them suspiciously. She pointed toward a one-story house with plywood over the window that had a surprisingly well-manicured lawn. A clean, freshly waxed Chevrolet four-by-four was parked in the driveway. "Shots from there, scared the *shit* outta me." The woman twirled her dry, broken hair around one finger. "You gotta tell 'em to *stop* that shit," she added. "Jesus *fuck*."

"All right," Ringley said. "We'll take care of this."

"Yeah yeah," the woman said to Ringley as she eyed Larsen's badge.

"Officer Ringley," Larsen said, "why don't you stay with the witness, I'll check this out. Bet someone shot out his Magnavox over the way Judge Judy was lookin' at him."

"Right," Ringley said. "Be careful and keep your ears on. Vest?"

"Always," Larsen replied, tugging the Kevlar down toward his waist. Vests always rode up on him, but they beat getting filled full of holes. He unfastened the snap on his holster, but didn't draw—no point letting some nut job think he was charging in, ready to shoot. He only drew the Glock to his chest once he reached to door, and rapped a fist on the hard wood three times.

"Police!" he bellowed. "Open up!"

Now the worst part of any blind call, Larsen thought. The few seconds where an officer has no idea whether he's about to be decapitated by a shotgun or greeting with a plate of cookies and a smile.

The blonde man who answered the door proved to be an unexpected third option. Clad in a long white bathrobe like the kind Larsen had only seen in expensive hotels, he appeared to have just gotten out of the shower. He was slim and well-manicured, two adjectives Larsen had never used to describe anyone in his life. He was at least half a head taller than Larsen, but raised both hands in surprise at Larsen's drawn weapon.

"Officer," the man said. "Can I help you?"

"Will you step outside for a moment, sir?"

"I would be happy to. May I put my hands down?"

"Soon," Larsen said. "Is there anyone inside with you, sir?" All he could see was a darkened house.

"No. I was afraid this might happen. Is this about the gunshot?"

"Is there anyone inside?" Larsen said. "I'm not asking again."

"Again, no," the man insisted. "But I believe I can explain. If I join you on the stoop, may I put my hands down?"

"I got you covered," Ringley called from the car. The witness appeared to have fled.

The man explained that he was only staying in the house for a few months—he'd inherited it from an uncle, and had just started getting it ready for sale. The gunshot had happened when he mistakenly thought a neophyte like himself could still disassemble and clean a gun for resale on an online auction site.

The guy was boring, an academic who belonged in a lecture hall or art museum, not a firing range. Besides, Larsen thought, eyeing Ringley's tits, most every other car was at a fire or trying to stop new ones right now. He and his new partner had just enough time to get into some trouble.

Larsen took a step back, holstered his sidearm. "Sir," he said. "Thank you for your time. I don't believe we have any problems here so long as we don't have to come back. You understand, Mister...?"

"David. Eric David."

"All right. You take care, now." Larsen waited until the man returned inside the house, then strolled back to the patrol car wearing a lopsided grin and the beginnings of a hard-on.

He soon saw he hadn't underestimated the thrill of a potentially dangerous call on a rookie officer. When he made his proposition after returning to the car, she grinned and placed a hand on his thigh. Larsen floored it, tearing away from the curb and onto Twelfth Avenue.

Larsen found himself grinning as he accelerated toward a red light. He almost didn't stop, then couldn't stop, and had to wrench the wheel to the right to avoid hitting a truck that flew crossways through the intersection. Ringley slid across the seat, rolling into his lap. "We should go back to the station," she said, pressing her cheek into his swelling crotch.

"Back to the station," Larsen said. He downshifted, wrenched the wheel right again, and entered a narrow alley between Twelfth and Thirteenth. Larsen accelerated as Ringley sat up with a laugh, reaching over for his belt.

Tweakers and junkies, get out of the way.

It was neither a tweaker nor a junkie who emerged into the alley wearing only a pair of white briefs, flip-flops, and a pair of black garbage bags over one shoulder. It was David Parsons, who had not told the whole truth about his name. He would not get the chance to correct the record. The cruiser's right front bumper caught the killer in the left thigh, shattering it instantly before driving the shards through his right leg. Moments later his entire pelvis and spine were pulverized, and David's head and torso whiplashed into the hood and windshield of the police cruiser. His ribs caved in, sharp bone pierced his heart, and the top of his head embedded itself in the windshield directly in front of Ringley. His ruined skull burst open to shower her with brains and gore. Officer Ringley screamed.

Larsen slammed on the brakes, forgetting that neither of them had bothered with seatbelts. The sudden deceleration launched Ringley head first into the windshield. The collision was an implosion of flesh, bone and gray matter that blinded the horrified Larsen as the car entered a spin.

He might have been able to recover control of the cruiser if not for the alley's lone speed bump, which the cruiser struck at a ninety-degree angle in mid-slide. The car went airborne for a few dizzying moments, landed hard, and rolled three times before it came to rest on ruined wheels in a cloud of dust, smoke, and blood.

When the emergency responders arrived on the scene, already exhausted from dealing with several fires, they found the car had flattened several fences, garbage cans, gardens, and one unlucky raccoon. Two of the EMTs vomited before they were out of the ambulance. Officer Ringley's upper torso was nearly pulped, the lower half of her corpse hanging like a grisly decoration from the windshield. Larsen remained conscious a few minutes after help arrived. He nodded when they explained the steering wheel had crushed his entire torso below his heart, and that when they pulled him from the wreck he'd be dead within a minute. He died long before they had a chance to try.

"Most of David Parsons' body was strewn along the alley, except for a few sizable chunks left in the windshield of the cruiser. Far more baffling to investigators were the dismembered remains of Mitchell Lewis," a boy said, reading from his phone. His name was Howie, and he was a true crime buff. That's what he told his mom, and that's why she bought him subscriptions to *True Crime* and *Front Page Detective* even though he was only eleven.

Howie was reading this story off of a local blog with connections to the police department. The blog never spared the blood and guts. Two younger boys who clearly worshipped Howie sat next to him on the Twelfth Avenue curb the day after the accident. They could see the police tape from where they were sitting, which to Howie made the whole thing feel like an episode of *America's Most Wanted*.

One of the other boys coughed, and Howie stopped gazing wistfully at the crime scene and continued reading. "Lewis, the prime suspect in a bank robbery that triggered a tragic string of events which..." Howie paused, silently sounded out the next word, and continued. "Which *culminated* in several deaths and substantial property damage along the twelve hundred block south, was believed to have fled into the foothills overlooking Ocean Beach. The manhunt in that area has now been called off." Howie nodded sagely, as he often did when editorializing. "Smart. No need for a manhunt if you know where the body is."

"What's it say about his condition? Wasn't he *pulped*?" one of the younger boys interrupted. He had dark eyes and hair, and had been amazed that someone could be turned into something like the orange juice he drank every morning.

"Ah-ha," Howie said. "That's the thingus, dingus." He punched the younger kid on the arm. "Something weird about *this* body. Not pulped." He picked up his phone again to read. "The corpse, though subject to some damage in the accident, had previously been surgically disassembled—that means taken apart, like a Lego dude or something—according to forensic reports."

"So what, he was dead already?" the other boy asked. Unlike his friend, this boy was blonde, pale, and green around the gills. He had already thrown up when the condition of Ringley's body had been described in vivid detail.

"Very good," Howie said, and the green boy's color started to return to normal. "I mean, *duh*, dickweed," he added, and the sick boy's complexion settled on a mottled blotchy red in a field of pea soup. "Of course he was already dead. That means the guy who lived there killed him. And it says here? The cops haven't found the money the chopped-up guy stole."

"Yeah?" the pulp enthusiast asked. "So you think what, we can find it?"

"Why not?" Howie asked. "We can hoist Puke through a window. The money has to be in there. Nobody lives in that house. He can't have been in there long."

"Don't call me Puke," said the boy who would not answer to another name for the rest of his admittedly short life. "If you jerks can hoist me up there, I'll do it."

"I'll call you Puke," Howie said. "Puke and Pulp. Come on, all the cops in town are out trying to put things back together."

The house proved easy to break into, but very dark inside. The dim light from Howie's phone wasn't much help, but he had a book of matches he'd smuggled out of a drawer his parents didn't think he knew about. He struck a match on the box and gasped at the sudden movement of deep shadows in the empty house. Spying a fat, scented candle in the center of a small table, he lit the wick before the match burned his thumb.

"Howie," Puke said. "I smell something awful. Like stinky diapers mixed with that dead possum from last summer."

"Shut up," Howie said. But he added, "I do too. It's just a dead rat." He lit a few more candles, which someone had been smart enough to place at regular intervals around the room. Weird, thought Howie. Like he wasn't the first one who had needed to light things up in here.

Everyone on the twelve hundred block knew no one had lived here for years. And the dust looked as old as Howie's grandma.

It was Pulp who found the duffel bag. While Howie and Puke kept focusing on trap doors and cupboards, Pulp thought to try the bedroom. His screams were terrified at first, but soon gave way to yelps of glee. The other two boys closed in on the sound.

The woman who had once owned this house must have died long before any of them were born. Someone, maybe the blonde man, had dressed her in old-fashioned clothes from back in the Eighties. Her shirt had once been white, and Howie thought he could read the word 'RELAX' in really tall letters. She looked all shriveled, like a mummy, and even her shiny black hair was covered in dust. The only thing that looked strange was her neck. There was a long, deep cut across her throat, covered in crusty brown and black blotches.

Next to the woman and in sharp contrast to her careful repose sat the big black duffel bag. The seams on one side of the zipper had ripped and Howie could see stacks, and stacks, and *stacks* of money. More money than Howie thought even existed in the world. All of it right there. He was eleven years old, but he'd been around long enough to know money bought happiness. And there were so many *other* things it could buy, which also led to happiness. His mother could stop working. His grandma could move out, get an apartment. He could buy a car. No, a motorcycle. *Then* a car.

All the Jolly Ranchers he wanted. Every Transformer. In the world.

"What do we do, Howie?" asked Pulp, his eyes wide. "What if someone wants it back? What if somebody arrests us?"

Howie didn't answer. Puke spoke up. "No one knows. They haven't searched the whole place yet. No electricity. They're probably waiting. Fires. No rush."

"No rush," Howie said softly. He reached into his pocket, and his hand closed over his most valued possession—a gift from his grandfather that his mom had only let him start carrying it when he turned eleven. A Barlow pocket knife with two blades, one big and one small. Just like Pulp and Puke.

"So... we're gonna share, right?" Pulp asked. "I mean, three musketeers, right? That's us? I mean, look at it, Howie! We're rich! It's like *The Goonies*! What are you going to do with your share?"

"Keep it," Howie said. He kicked the younger boy in the chest, slamming him against the back wall. A hand lashed out, unnaturally quick, seizing the other boy by the neck. Both blades flashed red and gold in the candlelight before an errant jet of fresh blood snuffed the candle out.

ABOUT THE AUTHORS

Brent Michael Kelley lives in the countryside north of Tomahawk, Wisconsin, with his wife Keri, their son Jordy, and a small zoo of strange animals. He assures you he is not building an army of clone-bots at a secret bunker in the forest. His rivals may insist otherwise, but they are all madmen, bent on world domination. Not Brent, though. Nope. In addition to short stories, he writes about his pal Chuggie, the drunken and travel-worn embodiment of drought. Chuggie and the Desecration of Stagwater is available now, and the next Chuggie adventure is coming soon. Brent keeps his readers up to date at www.brentmichaelkelley.com.

Kurt Fawver writes speculative fiction for hungry minds and depraved souls. He has been published in numerous anthologies and magazines, all of which you should rush out and purchase this instant. In an equally imaginative vein, he teaches English courses at the University of South Florida while earning his Ph.D. in literature. You can find him online at www.kurtfawver.com or www.facebook.com/kfawver.

Christian Larsen grew up in Park Ridge, Illinois and graduated from Maine South High School in 1993. He has worked as an English teacher, radio personality, newspaper reporter, and a printer's devil, and has been published by *What Fears Become* (Imajin Books), *A Feast of Frights* (The Horror Zine Books), and *The Ghost IS the Machine* (Post Mortem Press).

Christian received his bachelor of science in broadcast journalism from the University of Illinois and studied secondary English education at National-Louis University. He lives with his wife and two sons in the fictional town of Northport, Illinois. Follow him on Twitter @exlibrislarsen or visit exlibrislarsen.com.

Deported from England for stealing a load of bread and a gentleman's silk 'andkerchief, **Phil Hickes** currently resides in a New Zealand penal colony where he works as an advertising copywriter. In his spare-time he enjoys prowling the foggy streets in a hansom cab, with top hat, frock coat and surgical bag, laughing maniacally for no apparent reason. You can find him by searching 'Phil Hickes' on Amazon and read his bland but well intentioned tweets @hickesy.

Wednesday Lee Friday is a Michigan fiction writer, horror fan, and zombie defense strategist. Her horror novels include A Stabbing for Sadie and Kiss Me Like You Love Me— available in paperback and on all major ePub formats. She holds a B.A. in theatre and broadcasting from Olivet College, and produces the free audiobook podcast Take a Stab at THIS, available at iTunes. Wednesday Lee Friday eats true crime for breakfast, knows enough Dothraki to buy a horse, and is a contributing editor at Zombie Zone News. Catch up with her on Facebook, or at her website: www.wednesdayleefriday.com.

Garrett Cook is a small press novelist in the Bizarro movement. His latest book is Jimmy Plush, Teddy Bear Detective from Eraserhead Press. When he's not writing Bizarro, he's editing *Imperial Youth Review*, a magazine coming soon from Dog Horn Publishing in the UK and singing in the band Mayonnaise Jenkins and the Former Kings of the Delta Blues.

Lizz-Ayn Shaarawi primarily writes screenplays but also enjoys creating short stories. She's a fan of things that go bump, even if it's not the night.

Andrew Dombalagian is a writing tutor and author who lives, works, and dreams in the Philadelphia area. His other fiction has appeared through *Innsmouth Free Press*, including more exploits of the Nightcroft family. Andrew chases away monsters with the help of his fiancee, Ellen, and their three cats.

John Jasper Owens and **Lydia Ondrusek** have been all up in each other's business for years now. Despite that, "Best Laid Plans" is their first co-authored publication. John's work can be found in many places, including A Capella Zoo and the Day Terrors anthology. Lydia's most lately been in *GUD* and the recent BEAST WITHIN 2 anthology. Google them, they like it. It tickles.

Eric J. Guignard writes dark fiction from his office in southern California. His most recent writing credits include *Stupefying Stories Magazine*, +Horror Library+ Vol. 5 (Cutting Block Press), The *Horror Zine Magazine*, and *Indie Gypsy*. He's a member of the Horror Writer's Association and the Greater Los Angeles Writer's Society. Although his passion is for fiction, he's also a published essayist and editor, including this year's acclaimed collection, Dark Tales of Lost Civilizations. Look for the next anthology, After Death..., to be released in Spring, 2013. Visit Eric at: www.ericjguignard.com or at his blog: www. ericjguignard.blogspot.com.

Andrew Stockton lives in the Land of Song, Castles and Rain (though sadly not in that order) Wales, with his lovely wife and two fabulous daughters. Likes: writing, family life, soccer, listening to music. Dislikes: prejudice, impatience (except in himself), parsnips— oh yes, and lists. In the last 18 months or so he has had stories published in Ethereal Tales magazine, in *First Time Dead*— an anthology of horror themed short stories— and has stories due to appear in forthcoming issues of *Dark Tales* and *Isotropic Fiction* magazines. He also writes for a couple of UK soccer-related websites.

Cory J. Herndon is the author of several novels, including The Living Dead (writing as T.H. Lain), Lorwyn (co-writing with Scott McGough), The Fifth Dawn, and Ravnica: City of Guilds. He lives in Southern California with wife S.P. Miskowski and cats Bayliss & Remo. All four are fond of food, sleep, and pieces of string.

ABOUT THE EDITORS

LS Murphy lives the Greater St. Louis area where watches Cardinals baseball, reads every book she can find, and weaves tales for young adults and adults. Her debut YA novel Reaper will be released in January 2013. She can be found at LSMurphy.com and followed on Twitter: http://twitter.com/#!/LSMurphy.

Kate Jonez writes dark fantasy fiction. Her novel Candy House should be released into the wild in 2013 and her latest novel Bombay Island is searching for a home. She is chief editor at Omnium Gatherum, a small press dedicated to providing unique dark fantasy fiction in print, ebook and audio formats. To learn more about Omnium Gatherum visit the publisher's website at http://omniumgatherume-dia.com. When she's not writing editing or doing her publishing chores, she reads, takes photos, investigates odd and obscure historical stuff and collect things in jars.

www.ingramcontent.com/pod-product-compliance
Lightning Source LLC
Chambersburg PA
CBHW072144170626
46813CB00004BA/1657